KÁLMÁN MIKSZÁTH

St Peter's Umbrella

TRANSLATED BY B. W. WORSWICK

WOODCUTS BY ZOLTAN PEREI

THE FOLIO SOCIETY LONDON 1966

This translation by B. W. Worswick is used
by kind permission of the Hutchinson Publish-
ing Group and the revisions made by István
Fekete by kind permission of Corvina Press,
Budapest.

Printed and bound by
W. & J. Mackay & Co. Ltd, Chatham, Kent
Set in Monotype Bulmer 11 on 12 point

Contents

Introduction

Nationalist aspirations and the growth of an indigenous culture go hand in hand; they are mutually supporting, each an inspiration to the other. In Hungary, a history of Hapsburg oppression and of germanophobia—let alone a history of wars, both internal and external, and of consequent exhaustion—meant that the ground was left barren in which any specifically Magyar culture might have taken root. With the exception of a brief flowering of patriotic, lyric poetry, which coincided with the peasants' uprising under Rakoczi, Magyar literature remained in a purely embryo state until the end of the eighteenth century.

In the transformation that then began to take place the first two protagonists of stature were George Bessenyei (1747–1811), a disciple of Voltaire and an apostle of French enlightenment, and Ferenc Kazinczy (1759–1831), who initiated the movement for the reform of the Hungarian language, and was virtually dictator of the literary scene until 1822. With the establishment, in 1830, of the Academy of Sciences—which fostered not only science, but also language and literature—and the creation of the Kisfaludy Society—after two brothers, one a romantic poet and the other a nationalist playwright—the progress of development was considerably accelerated.

This upsurge of nationalism was equally apparent in other fields. When Francis I was forced to summon the Diet in 1825, Count Széchenyi, a leading figure in the movement, addressed it in Magyar and not in Latin—an apparently minor innovation in itself, but a major portent of the trend. Very shortly afterwards the nationalist spirit began to focus its aspirations in Lajos Kossuth, who became the outstanding figure behind the 1848 Hungarian revolution and the short-lived declaration of Hungarian independence the following year. Meanwhile, between 1839 and 1847, the expatriate Franz Liszt published his *Mélodies Hongroises*, drawing his inspiration from the folk music of the gipsy bands.

The failure of the revolution inevitably damped the fires, but it did not put them out. After 1850 growth may have been slower, but it was a steady, sober growth, the extent of which is reflected in the fact that though, in 1830, there were only ten Magyar periodical publications, by 1880 there were almost four hundred, and by 1895 the total had topped the eight hundred mark.

Because of his immense output, the literary field was for many years dominated by Mór Jókai (1825–1904), a romantic novelist with close affinities to Sir Walter Scott, Jules Verne, and Alexandre Dumas. His vivid narrative imagination was such that, during his lifetime, he completely overshadowed his contemporaries, even despite the fact that his novels show an almost total absence of characterization. Among those whose achievements were never fully recognized while Jókai was flooding the market was Kálmán Mikszáth. Today, however, it is accepted that Mikszáth's talents were of a far higher order than Jókai's, and that it was he who raised Hungarian prose writing to a new level, so marking the transition between the nineteenth and twentieth centuries.

Kálmán Mikszáth was born in 1847, the son of small landowners who farmed a few acres in northern Hungary, not far from the Czechoslovak border. After leaving the local grammar school, Mikszáth went to Budapest to study law and, though he failed to take his degree, it was during this period that he first started to write. In 1871 he returned to his home county of Nógrád to work in the sheriff's office, but he soon gave that up to become an articled clerk. In 1873, without her parents' knowledge, he married his employer's daughter, Ilona Mauka, and returned to Budapest, determined to make writing his career.

Success was by no means immediate and acute poverty first made his wife ill, then drove her to return to her family, and finally, in 1875, led to a divorce. Mikszáth managed to keep himself alive by writing articles and short stories for various Budapest newspapers until, in 1878, he went to Szeged, where he joined the staff of the local daily paper. After two and a half years there he returned to Budapest to work on the literary periodical *Ország-Világ*, and the following year he joined the editorial board of the newly founded *Pesti Hírlap*. The turning-point had now been reached and shortly afterwards, in 1881, he achieved his first success with *Tót atyafiak* (Our Slovak Kinsmen), a volume of short stories about peasant life. This success was followed up the next year with a further volume, *A jó palócok* (The Good Palóc People). Now that his reputation was established his former wife could take a brighter view of the prospects and, in 1882, she remarried him and bore him two sons, both of whom became minor writers, but were only pale shadows of their father.

Elected a liberal member of parliament in 1887 and a member of the Academy of Sciences in 1889, Mikszáth went on producing novels and volumes of short stories one after the other with unabated success, and his prolific output continued until his death in 1910.

The influences of his childhood, the countryside in which he grew up—very like that which forms the background to *St Peter's Umbrella*—and his early knowledge and love of the rich folk culture he found around him, all played a major part in Mikszáth's artistic development. As he himself said in later life: 'I learnt to tell a story not from the writers of novels but from the Hungarian peasants'. It is in his ability to fuse colloquial speech and the telling of anecdote into a work of art, in his skill in reflecting the realities of daily life in a way that both delights and amuses the reader, that raises Mikszáth to a position of eminence not only in Hungarian but also in European literature. That his works also reflect the social criticism of a liberal politician is equally true, but having made his point—the disgrace of poverty or the fecklessness of the gentry—he does not labour it. To amuse the reader is his prime purpose; focusing attention on the evils of the world is done by implication.

St Peter's Umbrella is Mikszáth's best-loved work. First published in 1895, it has, since then, been translated into eighteen other languages. The first English translation appeared in 1900 and forms the basis for this edition, though the revisions made by István Fekete for the Corvina Press in 1962 have also been incorporated.   R.B.C.

PART ONE

The Legend

- I -

Little Veronica is Taken Away

The schoolmaster's widow at Haláp was dead. When a schoolmaster dies there is little in it for the grave-diggers, but when his widow follows him, there is even less. And all this one had left was a goat, a goose she had been fattening, and a tiny girl of two. The goose ought to have been fattened only a week longer, but evidently the poor woman had not been able to hold out even that long. As far as the goose was concerned she had died too soon, for the child it was too late. In fact, she ought never to have been born. It would have been better had the woman been summoned away by the Lord when her poor husband was. (Dear me, what a splendid voice that man had!)

The child was born after its father's death, well within the proper time, a month—or it may have been two months—later. I ought to have my tongue torn out of my head if I were to say anything improper. I don't say so and I don't think so. The mother was a good, honest woman, but what did she have to have that baby for? It would have been easier for her to die with the child under her heart than leave it behind in this world alone. Besides, it did not seem quite right—may the Lord not put it against her!—for they already had a son, a priest, a very good son on the whole, only it was a pity he could not help his mother a bit; but he was very poor himself, and lived a long way off up in Slovakia, as curate to an old priest. But rumour has it that two weeks ago he had been presented with a living in a small village called Glogova, somewhere in the mountains between Selmecbánya and Besztercebánya. There was a man in Haláp, János Kapiczány, who had passed there once when he was driving some oxen to a fair, and he said it was a miserable little place.

And now the schoolmaster's widow must needs go and die, just when her son might have been able to help her a little. But no amount of talking would bring her back again, and I must say, for the honour of the inhabitants of Haláp, that they gave the poor soul a very decent funeral.

There was not quite enough money collected to defray the expenses, so they had to sell the goat to make up the sum; but the goose was left, though there was nothing for it to feed on, so it gradually got thinner and thinner, till it was its original size again; its slow wheezing gave way to normal breathing, and instead of waddling about in the awkward ungainly way it had done on account of its enormous size, it began to move with the brisk pace of its former days; in fact, its life had been saved by the loss of another. God in His wisdom by taking one life often saves another, for, believe me, senseless beings are entered in His book as well as sensible ones, and He takes, perhaps, as much care of them as of kings and princes.

The wisdom of God is great, but that of the Judge of Haláp was not trifling either. He ordered that after the funeral the little girl (Veronica was her name) was to spend one day at every house in the village in turns, and was to be looked after as one of the family.

'And how long is that to last?' asked the worried parish councillors.

'Until I deign to give orders to the contrary,' answered Judge Mihály Nagy shortly. And so things went on for ten days, until it was learned that Máté Billeghi and Ferenc Koczka decided to take their wheat to Besztercebánya to sell (for they had heard that the Jews down that way were not yet so sharp as in the neighbourhood of Haláp). This was a good chance for the Judge.

'Well,' he said, 'if you take your wheat there, you may as well take the child to her brother. Glogova must be somewhere that way.'

'Not a bit of it,' was the answer; 'it is in a totally different direction.'

'It must be up that way if I say so,' thundered out the Judge.

Billeghi and Koczka tried to get out of it, saying it was awkward for them, and out of their way. But it was of no use; when the Judge ordered a thing, it had to be done. So one Wednesday they put the sacks of wheat into Billeghi's cart, and on the top of them a basket containing Veronica and the goose, for the latter was, of course, part of the inheritance. The good folks of the village had made shortbread and biscuits for the little orphan to take with her on her journey out into the great world, and they also filled a stout bag with dried pears and plums; and as the heavy cart drove off many of them shed tears for the poor little waif who had no idea where they were taking her to, but only saw, smiling, that when the gee-gees began to move she still kept her place in the basket on top of a sack, and only the houses, gardens, fields and trees seemed to move, coming up to meet her!

- II -

Glogova as it Used to be

Not only the worthy Kapiczány had seen Glogova; the writer of these pages has also been there. It is a miserable little place tucked away in a narrow valley between barren mountains. There is not a decent road for miles around, much less a railway. Nowadays they say there is some sort of a rickety old engine, with a carriage or two attached, that plies between Besztercebánya and Selmecbánya, but it does not pass anywhere near Glogova. It will take at least five hundred years to bring Glogova up to that pitch of civilization other villages have reached.

The soil is poor, a sort of clay, and very little will grow there except oats and potatoes, and even these have to be coaxed from the ground. A soil like that cannot be spoken of as 'Mother Earth'; it is more like a mother-in-law. It is full of pebbles, and has broad cracks here and there, on the borders of which grows a kind of whitish feather grass like grey hairs on the chin of some old wizened gammer.

Is the soil too old? Why, it cannot be older than any other soil, but its strength has been used up more rapidly. Down below in the plain they have been growing nothing but grass for thousands of years, but up here enormous oak-trees used to grow, so it is no wonder that the soil has lost its strength. Poverty and misery reign here, and yet the place has an indefinable charm and poetic quality. The giant rocks that look down on them lend beauty to the ugly peasant huts. It would be a sin to build castles there, which, with their overornamented towers, would hide those wild-looking rocks.

The perfume of the elder and juniper fills the air, but there are no other flowers, except here and there in some of the tiny gardens, a mallow, white or purple, which a barefooted, fair-haired Slovak girl tends, and waters from a broken jug.

I see the little village before me as it was in 1873 when I was there last; I see its small houses, the tiny gardens sown partly with clover, partly with maize, with here and there a plum-tree, its branches supported by props. For the fruit-trees at least did their duty, as though they had decided to make up to the poor Slovaks for the poverty of their harvest.

When I was there the priest had just died, and the district magistrate and I had to take an inventory of his possessions. There was nothing worth speaking of, a few bits of furniture, old and well worn, and a few shabby cassocks. But the villagers were sorry to lose the old priest.

'He was a good man,' they said, 'but he had no idea of economy, though, after all, he had not very much to economize with.'

'Why don't you pay your priest better?' my principal rebuked them. And a big burly Slovak answered jauntily, shoving his pouch further up his stomach:

'The priest is not our servant but the servant of God, and every master must pay his own servant.'

After making the inventory, and whilst the coachman was harnessing his horses, we walked across the road to have a look at the school, for my companion was very fond of posing as a patron of learning. The school-house was small and low, with a simple, thatched roof. Only God Himself could boast a shingled roof in all

Glogova, but even His house was very simply built, and there was no tower to it, only a small belfry at one side.

The schoolmaster was waiting for us in the courtyard. If I remember rightly, his name was György Majzik. He was a strong, robust-looking man, with an interesting, intelligent face, and a plain straightforward way of speaking which immediately awoke a feeling of friendship in one. He took us in to see the children; the girls sat on one side, the boys on the other, all as tidy and clean as can be. They rose on our entrance, and in a singing voice said:

'Vitajte páni, vitajte!' (Good morning, honoured sirs!)

My companion put a few questions to the rosy, round-faced children, who stared at us with their large brown eyes. They all had brown eyes. The questions were, of course, not difficult—if God were one, what was the name of this country, and the like—but they caused the children an amount of serious thinking. However, the magistrate was indulgent, and he only patted the schoolmaster on the back and said:

'I am quite contented with their answers, my friend.'

The schoolmaster bowed and then, with his head held high, accompanied us out to the road.

'They are pretty children,' said the magistrate lightly, 'but how is it, *domine*, that they are all so much alike?'

The schoolmaster looked a little confused, and then his healthy, ruddy cheeks became suffused with frank joviality.

'Well, you see, sir, in the summer all the men of Glogova go down to the plains to work, and I am quite alone here till the autumn.' (A mischievous smile played around the corners of his mouth.) 'Do you understand, sir?'

'And how many years have you been here?'

'Fourteen years, sir. I see from your question that you understand.'

I remember the little dialogue to this day when thinking of Glogova. Once in the carriage we referred to it again, and had a good laugh about it, and the magistrate often told the story at home as a good joke.

About two years afterwards we heard that a young priest had gone to Glogova in place of the one who had died. His name was János Bélyi; and I remember the magistrate to have remarked:

'Well, the schoolmaster won't be alone now in the summer!'

- III -

The New Priest at Glogova

The new priest had arrived in the only cart the villagers had at their disposal. Two cows with crumpled horns were harnessed to it, and on the way Péter Szlávik, the sacristan, stopped to milk them, and then offered some of the milk to the young priest.

'It's very good milk,' he said, 'especially Bimbó's. Real nectar, it is.'

The reverend father's luggage was not bulky; it consisted of a plain wooden box, a bundle of bed-clothes, two walking-sticks, and some long pipes tied together with string. As they passed through the various villages the sacristan was often chaffed by the inhabitants.

'Well,' they called out to him, 'couldn't you find a better conveyance than that for your new priest?'

Whereupon the sacristan tried to justify his fellow villagers by saying, with a contemptuous look at the luggage in the cart:

'It's good enough, I'm sure. Why, a calf a month old could draw those things.'

But if he had not brought much with him in the way of worldly goods, the reverend János Bélyi did not find much either in his new parish, which appeared to be going to rack and ruin. The relations of the dead priest had taken away every stick they could lay hands on, and had only left a dog, his favourite. It was a dog such as one sees every day, as far as his shape and coat were concerned, but he was now, on account of his ill-mannered ways, in a very unpleasant position. After midday his gluttony would send him wandering from house to house in the village, slinking into the kitchens; for his master had been in the habit of dining every day with one or other of his parishioners, and had always taken his dog with him.

The dog's name was Vistula, but his master need not have gone so far to find the name of a river, when the Biela Voda flowed right through the meadows outside the village. The dog had already begun bitterly to feel that he and the priest together had been better received than he alone, though, until now, he had always imagined, with his canine philosophy, that his master had in reality been eating more than his share of the food. Yes, but then he had lent all the prestige! Now Vistula was turned out of the kitchens before he could go about his business, and all he would get once in a while was a good chiding.

So altogether he was in a very miserable, lean condition when the new priest arrived. The sacristan had shown him his new home, with its four bare walls, its garden overgrown with weeds, its empty stable and sty. The poor young priest smiled.

'And is that all mine?' he asked.

'All of it, everything you see here,' was the answer, not spoken without humour, 'and this dog, too.'

'Whose dog is it?'

'It belonged to the poor dead priest, God rest his soul. We thought of killing the poor useless beast, but no one dares to, for they say that maybe his old master is watching from Heaven and his spirit would come back and haunt us.'

The dog was looking at the young priest in a melancholy, almost tearful way; perhaps the sight of the cassock awoke sad memories in him.

'I will keep him,' said the priest, and stooping down he patted the dog's lean back. 'At all events there will be some living thing near me.'

'That will be quite right,' said the sacristan with a grin. (For peasants delight in poking fun at priests.) 'One must make a beginning, though one generally gets something worth watching first, and then looks out for a watchdog. But it doesn't matter if it is the other way round.'

János Bélyi smiled (he had a very winning smile, like a girl's), for he saw that old Vistula would not have much to do, in fact would be quite like a private gentleman among his fellows.

All this time people had been arriving in the yard to have a look at the new priest; the women kept at a distance, and said: 'Dear me! so young and already in holy orders!'

The men went up and shook hands with him, saying: 'Welcome to Glogova! You will like it here.'

An old woman called out, 'You may be with us till your death!'

The older women admired his looks, and remarked what a pretty woman his mother must have been.

In fact, the new priest seemed to have taken everyone's fancy, and he spoke a few kindly words with the older people, and then said he was tired, and went across to the schoolmaster's, for he was to live there for a time till he could get his own place a bit straight, and until he saw some signs of an income.

Only a few of the more important villagers accompanied him there, those well informed in church affairs: Péter Szlávik, the sacristan; Mihály Gongoly, the nabob of Glogova; and the miller, György Klincsok. He began to question them on vain earthly matters, and took out his note-book, in order to make notes as to what his income was likely to be.

'How many inhabitants are there in the village?'

'A little short of five hundred.'

'And how much do they pay the priest?'

The good men began to reckon out accurately how much wood

they had to give, how much corn, and how much 'zlevka'.* The young priest looked more and more serious as they went on.

'That is very little,' he said sadly. 'And what are the fees?'

'Oh, they are large enough,' answered Klincsok, always well informed. 'At a funeral it depends on the dead person, at a wedding it depends on the people to be married (for they are pretty generous on that occasion as a rule), but at a christening one florin is paid! I'm sure that's something, isn't it?'

'And how many weddings are there in a year?'

'Oh, that depends on the potato harvest. Plenty of potatoes, plenty of weddings. The harvest decides it; but as a rule there are at least four or five.'

'That is not many. And how many deaths occur?'

'That depends on the quality of the potato harvest. If the potatoes are bad, there are many deaths; if they are good, there are fewer deaths, for we are not such fools as to die then. Of course, now and then a falling tree in the woods strikes one or the other dead; or a cart lands in a ditch, and the driver is killed. You may reckon a year with eight deaths a good one as far as you are concerned.'

'But they don't all belong to the priest,' said the nabob of Glogova, smoothing back his hair haughtily.

'Why, how is that?' asked the priest, somewhat taken aback.

'Many of the people here never come to be buried in the cemetery at all. The wolves eat them up without ever announcing it in the parish.'

'And some kick the bucket in summer in other parts of the country,' György Klincsok added, 'and all we get is some sort of a note about it addressed to the Judge.'

'It is a bad look-out,' said the priest. 'But the parish fields, what about them?'

Now they all wanted to speak at once, but Klincsok pulled the sacristan aside, and stood up in front of the servant of God.

---

* 'Zlevka' is the wine due to the priest from the vine-growers. Collected in a common vessel, it surely is a strange beverage. (K. M.)

'Fields?' he said. 'Why, you can have as much land as you like. If you want a hundred acres . . .'

'What, one hundred acres!' shouted Klincsok with enthusiasm. 'Five hundred if you like; we can't be so mean as to stint our priest of land!'

The priest's countenance began to clear, which the wicked Szlávik could not long endure.

'The fact is,' he began, 'the boundaries of the pasture-lands of Glogova are not well defined to this day. There is no proper land register; there was some arrangement made with regard to drawing one up, but in 1823 there was a great fire here, and all our documents were burnt. So everyone takes as much of the land as he and his family can till. Each man ploughs his own field, and when it is about used up he looks out a fresh bit of land. So half the ground is always unused, of course the worse part, into which it is not worth while putting any work.'

'I see,' sighed the priest, 'and that half belongs to the church.'

It was not a very grand look-out, but by degrees he got used to the idea of it, and if unpleasant thoughts would come cropping up, he flushed them down with a prayer. When praying, he was on his own ground, a field which always brought forth fruit; he could reap there at any minute all he was in need of—patience, hope, comfort, content. He set to work to get his house in order, so that he could at least be his own master. A curate knows how good that is. Luckily he had found in the next village an old school friend, Tamás Urszinyi, a big, broad-shouldered man, plain-spoken, but kind-hearted, who helped him out with a small loan.

'Glogova is a wretched hole,' he said. 'Not every place can be the Bishopric of Nyitra, but whose fault is it? Lean flock, lean shepherd. However, you will have to put up with it as it is. Daniel was worse off in the lions' den, and after all these are only sheep.'

'Which have no wool,' remarked the reverend, smiling.

'They have wool, but you have not the shears.'

In a few days he had furnished his house with the money he had borrowed of his friend, and one fine autumn afternoon he was able to take possession of his own house. Oh, how delightful it was to arrange things as he liked! What pleasant dreams he would have lying in his own bed, on pillows made by his own mother! He thought over it all when he lay down to sleep, and before going to sleep he counted the corners of the room so as to be sure and remember his dreams.*

He did remember his dream the next morning, and it was a very pleasant one. He was chasing butterflies in the fields outside his native village, looking for birds' nests, playing games with the boys and girls, having a quarrel with Pál Szabó, and he was just winning the fight when someone tapped at the window outside.

The priest awoke and rubbed the sweet dream out of his eyes. It was morning, the sun was shining into the room.

'Who is it?' he called out.

'Open the door, Jankó!'

Jankó! Who was calling him Jankó? It seemed to him as though it were one of his old schoolfellows, from whom he had just parted in his dream.

He jumped out of bed and ran to the window.

'Who is it?' he repeated.

'It is I,' was the answer, 'Máté Billeghi from your old home. Come out, Jankó; no, I mean, of course, please come out, your reverence. I've brought something.'

The priest dressed hastily. His heart was beating fast with a kind of presentiment that he was to hear bad news. He opened the door into the yard and stepped out under the eaves.

'Here I am, Mr Billeghi; what have you brought me?'

But Mr Billeghi had left the window and gone back to the cart, where he was unfastening the basket containing little Veronica and the goose. The horses hung their heads, and one of them tried to lie down, but the shaft was in the way, and when he tried the other side, he felt the harness cutting into his side, which reminded him that he was not in the stable, and a horse's honourable feeling

---

* The Hungarian peasants say that when you sleep in a room for the first time you must count the corners, then your dream is sure to come true. (Translator's note.)

will not allow of its lying down as long as it is harnessed to the cart. There must be something serious the matter to induce it to lie down in harness, for a horse has a high sense of duty. Máté Billeghi now turned round and saw the priest standing near him.

'Hallo, Jankó! My, what a lanky lad you are! How surprised your mother would be if she were alive! Bother this rope, I did make a firm knot in it!'

The priest took a step towards the cart, where Billeghi was still struggling with the knot. The words 'if she were alive' had struck him like a blow; his head began to swim, his legs to tremble.

'Are you speaking of my mother?' he stammered, paling. 'Is my mother dead?'

'Yes, poor woman, she has given up the ghost. But' (and here he took out his knife and began to cut the rope) 'here is your little sister, Jankó; that is, I mean, your reverence, my memory is as weak as a chicken's and I always forget whom I am talking to. I've brought your reverence's little sister; where shall I put her down?'

And with that he lifted up the basket in which the child was sleeping soundly with the goose beside her. The bird seemed to be acting the part of nurse to her, driving off the flies trying to settle on her little red mouth which seemed to attract them like honey.

The feeble autumn sunlight fell on the basket and the sleeping child, and Mr Billeghi was standing with his watery blue eyes fixed on the priest's face, waiting for a word or a sign from him.

'Dead!' he murmured after a time. 'Impossible. I had no feeling of it.' He put his hand to his head, saying sadly: 'No one told me, and I was not there at the funeral.'

'I was not there either,' said Mr Billeghi, as though that would console the other for his absence; and then added, as an after-thought, well-meaningly:

'God Almighty took her to Himself, He called her to His throne. He doesn't leave one of us here. Bother those frogs, now I've trodden on one!'

There were any amount of them in the weedy courtyard of the Presbytery; they came out of the holes in the damp walls of the old church to bask in the sun.

'Where shall I put the child?' repeated Mr Billeghi, but as he received no answer, he deposited her gently in the courtyard under the eaves.

The priest stood with his eyes fixed on the ground; it seemed to him as though the earth, with the houses and gardens, Mr Billeghi and the basket, were all running away, and only he was standing there, unable to move one way or the other. From the Ukrica woods in the distance there came a rustling of leaves, seeming to bring with it a sound that spoke to his heart, a sound that was like his mother's voice. He listened, trembling, and trying to distinguish the words, but as soon as he thought he had recognized one of his mother's phrases, some curious murmur would envelop their meaning. Silence. Then again but more distinctly now, his mother's voice came to him from the woods:

'János, János, take care of my child!'

But whilst János was occupied in listening to voices from a better land, good Máté Billeghi was getting tired of waiting, and, muttering something to himself about not getting even a friar's farthing for his trouble, he prepared to start. (Friar's farthing stands for 'thank you' in those parts.)

'Well, if that's the way they do things in these parts, I'll be off,' he grumbled, and cracking his whip he added: 'Good-bye, your reverence. Gee-up, Sármány!'

Father János still gave no answer, did not even notice in his grief what was going on around him, and the horses were moving on, Máté Billeghi walking beside them, for they had to go uphill now, and the good man was muttering to himself something about its being the way of the world, and only natural that if a chicken grows into a peacock, of course the peacock does not remember the time when it was a chicken. When he got up to the top of the hill he turned round and saw the priest still standing in the same place, and, making one last effort to attract his attention, he shouted:

'Well, I've given you what I was told to, so good-bye.'

The priest's senses at last returned from the paths in which they had been wandering, far away, with his mother. In his imagination he had looked her up first to spend with her once more the time he had eventually spent with her, then to spend with her the time of which distance had robbed him. He was kneeling and praying at her death-bed, and what his mother had in her mind then, what she was about to say then, her last sigh had been carried by the air to the wind and the wind made the woods resound it:

'Take care of my child, János!'

There is no need for the son to be at home to learn the last will of his dying mother. There was no need for János to have it written down or to be telegraphed to him; there were higher forces which communicated the fact to him.

János's first impulse was to run after Mr Billeghi and ask him to stop and tell him all about his mother, how she had lived during the last two years, how she had died, how they had buried her, in fact, everything. But the cart was a long way off by now, and besides, his eyes at that moment caught sight of the basket and its contents, and they took up his whole attention.

His little sister was still asleep in the basket. The young priest had never yet seen the child, for he had not been home since his father's funeral, and she was not born then; so he had only heard of her existence from his mother's letters, and they were always so short, so diffident. János went up to the basket and looked at the small rosy face. He found it bore a strong resemblance to his mother's and as he looked the face seemed to grow bigger, and with dazzled eyes he saw the features of his mother before him. God Almighty! What miracle, what mirage was this he saw? But the vision only lasted a minute, and the child's face was there again. If she would only open her eyes! But they were firmly closed, and the long eyelashes lay like dark silken fringes on her cheeks.

'And I am to take care of this little thing?' thought János and he felt unspeakable warmth rise about his heart. 'And I will take care of her. But how am I to do it? I have nothing to live on myself. What shall I do?'

He did as he always had done until now when he had been in doubt, and turned towards the church in order to say a prayer there. The church was open, and two old women were inside, whitewashing the walls.

So the priest did not go quite in to the altar where the two old women were busy, but knelt down before the wood-and-tin image of Christ that stood next to the holy-water basin at the entrance.

-IV-

The Umbrella and St Peter

Yes, he knelt down before Christ, he appealed to Jesus—to our Lord Jesus.

How lucky for mankind that there is a Jesus, a God who was a man. Of God I don't know what He is like, of Jesus I do. Jesus is somebody I know, somebody everyone knows. I know what He did, I know what He thought, I even know His face. My soul is content not because He is my Lord, but because He is an acquaintance of mine.

Two thousand years ago I had an acquaintance living on this planet—what a comforting thought! The people who were living then and the people who came after them had all gone to dust, from the dust grew grass, from the grass God knows what, but He, my acquaintance, has always lived, has always been and will always be.

When I am travelling in foreign lands, among foreign peoples, and I see other faces, other animals, other plants, even the sky is different, everything is different, so that in my utter, terrifying loneliness I fear that I am no longer in this world, then, all of a sudden, at the fringe of some human community I come across a crucifix which bears a man made of tin and bleeding from many wounds—a man who is an acquaintance of mine.

Ah, here He is! Here, too. And I am no longer lonely, I am no longer alone. I kneel down before Him and tell Him all that burdens my heart. The same way as this priest was doing.

The priest was kneeling before the image of Christ.

'Please help me, Lord Jesus,' Father János thought in his prayer. 'My mother is dead, my little sister has been brought to me, and I am to take care of her and bring her up. I am a poor priest who needs advice and help. I have never known what you do with a child. Ah, give me a saving idea, Jesus! And do throw me from Thy inexhaustible horn of plenty the means with which I shall be able to feed her and take care of her. Please work Thy miracles, Lord Jesus!'

The painted image of the Son of God seemed to be listening to the words of the priest's prayer. The sheaves of light and shade that came through the windows and were thrown back from the walls fell on the crucifix and played on it; and it seemed as if they were expressions of His face, and it seemed as if He were smiling amidst all His suffering, and were nodding His head as if to say: 'It's all right. I know all. I will intervene.'

Father János remained kneeling a long time and did not notice that, as it often happens in autumn, after a sweltering, almost unnatural heat, suddenly the sky was darkened—a storm was coming up. When he came out of the church it was pouring in torrents, and before long the small mountain streams were so swollen that they came rushing down into the village and the cattle in their fright ran lowing up and down the streets.

János's first thought was that he had left the child under the eaves, and it must be wet through. He ran home as fast as he could, but paused with surprise before the house. The basket was where he had left it, the child was in the basket, and the goose was walking about in the yard. The rain was still coming down in torrents, but on the child not a drop had fallen, for an immense red umbrella had been spread over the basket. It was patched and darned to such an extent that hardly any of the original stuff was left, and the border of flowers that trimmed it after the fashion of old times was all but invisible.

The young priest raised his eyes in gratitude to Heaven, and taking the child into his arms, showered it with kisses and carried it, under the red umbrella, into his room. The child's eyes were open now; they were a lovely blue, and gazed wonderingly into the priest's face.

'It is really a blessing,' he murmured, 'that the child did not get wet through; she might have caught her death of cold, and I could not even have given her dry clothes.'

But where had the umbrella come from? It was incomprehensible, for no one in the whole of Glogova did own a single umbrella.

In the neighbouring yards some peasants were digging ditches for the water to run into. His reverence asked them all in turn, had they seen no one with the child? No, they had seen the child, but as far as they knew no one had been near it. Old Widow Adamecz, who had run home from the fields with a shawl over her head, had seen something red and round, which seemed to descend from the clouds right over the child's head. Might she turn to stone that minute if it were not true, and she was sure the Virgin Mary herself had sent that contraption down from Heaven to the poor orphan child.

Widow Adamecz was a regular old gossip; she was fond of a drop of brandy now and then, so it was no wonder she sometimes saw more than she ought to have seen. The summer before, on the eve of the feast of Sts Peter and Paul, she had seen the skies open and Heaven was before her; she had heard the angels sing, as they passed in procession before God, sitting on a throne of carbuncles. And amongst them she had seen her grandson, Jankó Plachta, who had died three years before wearing that selfsame pretty red waistcoat she herself had made him shortly before his death. And she had seen many of the inhabitants of Glogova who had died within the last few years, passing slowly, solemnly to the sounds of the heavenly choirs, and they were all dressed in the clothes they had been buried in.

One can imagine that after that, when the news of her vision was spread abroad, she was looked upon as a very holy person indeed. All the villagers came to ask if she had seen their dead relations in the procession; this one's daughter, that one's father, and the other one's 'poor husband'.

They quite understood that such a miracle was more likely to happen to her than to anyone else, for a miracle had been worked on her poor dead father András Flinta, even though he had been looked upon in life as something of a thief. For when the high road had had to be made broader eight years before, they were obliged to take a bit of the cemetery in order to do it, and when they had opened the old man's grave, so as to bury him again, they saw with astonishment that he had a long beard, though five witnesses swore to the fact that at the time of his death he was clean-shaven through the good offices of Tamás Gundros, the cowherd.

So they were all quite sure that old Flinta was in Heaven, and having been an old cheat all his life he would, of course, manage even up above to leave the door open a bit now and then, so that his dear Agnes could have a peep at what was going on.

But Pál Kvapka, the bell-ringer, had another tale to tell. He said that when he had gone up the belfry to ring the clouds away, and had turned round for a second, he saw an old Jewish-looking individual shuffling along up the road towards the parsonage, and he had in his hands that immense red thing like a plate, which his reverence had found spread over the basket. Kvapka had thought nothing of it at the time, for he was sleepy, and the wind blew the dust in his eyes, but he could take an oath that what he had told them had really taken place. (And Pál Kvapka was a trustworthy person.) Others had also seen that Jewish-looking individual. He was old, tall, grey-haired, his back was bent, and he had a crook in his hand, and when, near the Pribils' well, the wind carried his hat away, they saw that he had a large bald patch at the crown of his head.

'I'll be hanged if he wasn't just like the picture of St Peter in the church,' said the sacristan, who had seen him without his hat. 'He was like him in every respect,' he repeated, 'except that he had no keys in his hand.'

From the Pribils' well he had cut across Stropov's clover-field, where the Krátkis' cow, which had somehow got loose, made a rush at the old Jew; in order to defend himself he struck at it with his stick (and from that time, you can ask the Krátki family if you don't believe it, the cow gave fourteen pints of milk a day, whereas they used to have the greatest difficulty in coaxing four pints from it).

At the other end of the village the old man had asked the miller's servant-girl which was the way to Lehota, and Erzsi had told him, upon which he had started on the footpath up the mountains. Erzsi said she was sure, now she came to think of it, that he had a glory round his head.

Why, of course it must have been St Peter! Why should it not have been? There was a time when he walked about on earth, with Our Lord Jesus, and there are many stories told still as to all he had done then. And what had happened once could happen again. The wonderful news spread from house to house that God had sent down from Heaven a sort of red-linen tent, to keep the rain off the priest's little sister, and had chosen St Peter himself for the mission.

Thereupon followed a good time for the child, she became quite the fashion in the village. The old women outdid one another in making cakes for her, also milk puddings, and various other delicacies. The reverend had nothing to do but answer the door all day, and receive from his visitors plates, dishes, or basins heaped with the choicest titbits and wrapped up in clean cloths. The poor young priest could not make out what was going on in his parish.

'Oh, your reverence, please, I heard your little sister had come, so I've brought her a trifle for her dinner; of course it might be better, but it is the best such poor folks as we can give. Our hearts are good, your reverence, but our flour might be better than it is, for that good-for-nothing miller burned it a bit the last time—at least that part of it which he did not keep for his own use. May I look at the little angel? They say she's a little beauty.'

Of course, his reverence allowed them all to look at her in turn, to pat her and smooth her hair; some of them even kissed her tiny feet.

The priest was obliged to turn away now and then to hide the tears of gratitude. He reproached himself, too, for his hard thoughts of the good villagers. 'How I have misjudged them!' he thought to himself. 'There are no better people in the world. And how they love me! It is amazing how much they love me!'

At tea-time Widow Adamecz appeared on the scene, though until now she had not troubled much about the new priest. She considered herself entitled to a word in the management of the ecclesiastical affairs of the village, and based her rights on the fact of her father having grown a beard in his grave, which, of course, sort of gave him a place among the saints at once.

'Your reverence,' she began, 'you will want someone to look after the child.'

'Yes, of course, I ought to have someone,' he replied, 'but the parish is poor, and . . .'

'Nobody is poor but the devil,' burst out Widow Adamecz, 'and he's poor because he has no soul. But we have souls. And after all, your reverence won't know how to dress and undress a child, nor how to wash it and plait its hair. And then she will often be hungry, and you can't take her across to the schoolmaster's each time. You must have someone to cook at home, your reverence. The bell-ringer is all very well for sweeping and tidying up a bit, but what does that numskull know about children?'

'True, true, but where am I to . . .'

'Where? And am I not here? The Lord created me for a priest's cook, being above suspicion as I am.'

'Yes, I dare say. But how am I to pay your wages?'

Widow Adamecz put her hands on her hips, and planted herself in front of Father János.

'Never mind about that, my dear. Leave it to God and to me. He will pay me for your reverence. I shall enter your service this evening, and shall bring all my saucepans and things with me.'

The priest was surprised a great deal, but even more astonished was his friend Urszinyi when he came over towards evening and the priest related the events of the day, and told him of Widow Adamecz's offer.

'What!' he exclaimed. 'Widow Adamecz? That old witch? And without payment? Why, János, a greater miracle never yet happened. An inhabitant of Glogova accepting God to stand surety for one! You seem to have bewitched the people.'

The priest only smiled, but his heart was full of gratitude. He also felt that a miracle had taken place; it was all so strange, so incomprehensible. But he guessed at the cause of the change. The prayer he had said kneeling on the cold church floor had been heard, and this was the answer. Jesus had collected the selfish souls of the villagers and had substituted for each a portion of His own. His holy breath was shining on their faces, on their behaviour. Yes, it really was a miracle!

He had not heard all the stories that were spread abroad about the red umbrella, and he only smiled at those that had come to his ears. It is true he did not understand himself how the umbrella came to be where he had found it; he was surprised at first, but had not thought any more about it, and had hung it on a nail in his room, so that if the owner asked for it he could have it at once, though it was not really worth sixpence, all told.

But the day's events were not yet done. Towards evening the news spread with lightning speed that the wife of the miller, the village nabob, had been drowned in the Biela Voda, which was immensely swollen from the amount of rain that had fallen. The unfortunate woman had crossed the stepping-stones in order to bring back her geese, which had strayed to the other side. She had brought back the gander and a black-tafted one, one under each arm, but as she was recrossing to fetch the other two, her foot slipped, and she fell into the raging stream. My goodness, in the morning there had been so little water there that a goat could have drank it all at one go, and by midday it was swollen to such an incredible extent that the poor woman was drowned in it, for there was no one about that might have pulled her out. They looked for her the whole afternoon in the cellar, in the loft, everywhere they could think of, until in the evening her body was washed ashore near Lehota. There some people recognized her, and a man was sent over on horseback to tell Mihály Gongoly of the accident. The tragedy caused great excitement in the village, and the people stood about in groups, talking of the event.

'Yes, God takes the rich ones, too,' they said.

György Klincsok came running in to the priest.

'There will be a grand funeral the day after tomorrow,' he exclaimed.

The sacristan appeared at the schoolmaster's in the hope of a glass of brandy to celebrate the event.

'Time for you to rack your brains,' he said; 'there is a fat little corpse, and they will expect some inspired verses.'

Two days later the funeral took place, and it was a long time since anything so splendid had been seen in Glogova. Mr Gongoly had sent for the priest from Lehota, too, for, as he said, why should not his wife have two priests to read the burial service over her. He sent all the way to Beszterce for the coffin, and they took the wooden cross that was to be put at the head of the grave to the carpenter at Kaponyica to have it painted black, with the name and the date of her drowning in white letters.

There were crowds of people at the funeral in spite of the bad weather, and just as the priest was starting in full canonicals, with all the little choir-boys in their clean surplices, it began to pour again; so Father János turned to Kvapka, the sacristan, and said:

'Run back as fast as you can and fetch the umbrella out of my room. You'll find it there right behind the cupboard.'

Kvapka turned and stared, how was he to know what an umbrella was?

'Well,' said Father János impatiently, 'if you like it better, fetch the large, round piece of red linen I found two days ago spread over my little sister.'

'Ah, that's different!'

The priest took shelter under the eaves of Péter Majgó's cottage until the fleet-footed Kvapka returned with the umbrella, which his reverence, to the great admiration of the crowd, with one sweeping movement of his hand spread out in such a fashion that it looked like a series of bats' wings fastened together. Then, taking hold of the handle, he raised it so as to cover his head, and walked on with stately step, without getting wet a bit; for the drops fell angrily on the strange tent spread over him, and, not being able to touch his reverence, fell splashing on to the ground. The umbrella was the great attraction for all people at the funeral, and they exchanged many whispered remarks about it.

'That's what St Peter brought,' they said.

Only the beautiful verses the schoolmaster had composed for the occasion distracted their attention for a while, and sobs broke forth as the various relations heard their names mentioned in the lines in which the dead woman was supposed to be taking leave of them:

'Here I am taking leave of my worthy neighbours; Pál Lajkó my cousin, György Klincsok my uncle.'

The whole of Pál Lajkó's household began to weep bitterly, and Mrs Klincsok explained rapturously:

'How on earth does he manage to compose such beautiful lines!'

Which exclamation inspired the schoolmaster with fresh courage, and, raising his voice, he continued haranguing the assembled friends and relations in the dead woman's name, not forgetting a single one, and there was not a dry eye amongst them.

For some time after they had buried Mrs Gongoly the grand doings at the funeral were still the talk of the place, and even at the funeral the old women—may God not set down their gossiping tongues against them—had picked out pretty Anna Tyurek as the successor of Mrs Gongoly, and felt sure it would not be long before the latter's noted 'mentyék' had an owner.*

The grave-diggers had hardly recovered from the large quanti-

---

* Every well-to-do Slovak peasant buys a long cloak of sheepskin for his wife; it is embroidered outside in bright colours, and inside is the long silky hair of the Hungarian sheep. It is only worn on Sundays and holidays, and is passed from one generation to another. It is called 'mentyék' by the Slovaks. (K. M.)

ties of brandy they had imbibed in order to drown their sorrow, when they had to dig a new grave; for János Srankó had followed Mrs Gongoly. In olden times he had been known to go gallivanting with Mrs Gongoly a great deal; and now it seemed as though they had arranged their departure from this world to take place at the same time. Just as one would have expected. Indeed, as gossip had it, Mrs Gongoly would sometimes disappear in the corn-field and then Srankó would crop up from nowhere and he, too, would disappear in the corn. Ah, that unholy corn! It grows so high that it conceals many a strange happening.

Again, the two shadows disappeared one after the other, but now in the corn-field of nothingness . . . They found Srankó dead in his bed, the morning after the funeral; he had apparently died of 'the thunderbolt of death', an apoplectic fit. Srankó was a well-to-do man, in fact a 'mágnács'.* He had three hundred sheep grazing in his meadows and several acres of land under plough, so he ought to have a grand funeral, too. And Mrs Srankó was no miser; she went herself to the schoolmaster, and then to the priest, and said she wished everything to be as it had been at Mrs Gongoly's funeral. Let it cost what it might, but the Srankós were not less than the Gongolys. She wished two priests to read the funeral service, and four choir-boys to attend in their best black cassocks, the bell was to toll at the time, and so on, and so on. Father János nodded his head contentedly.

'Very well, all shall be as you wish,' he said, and then proceeded to reckon out with chalk what it would cost.

'That's all right,' said Mrs Srankó, 'but please, your reverence, put the red thing in, too, and let us see how much more it will cost.'

'What red thing?'

'Why, what you held over your head at Mrs Gongoly's funeral. Oh! It was lovely!'

The young priest could not help smiling.

'But that is impossible!' he said.

---

* *The fifteen richest peasants in a Slovak village are called 'mágnács' or 'magnates'. (Translator's note.)*

Mrs Srankó jumped up, and planted herself before him, with her arms crossed.

'And why is it impossible I should like to know? My money is as good as the Gongolys', isn't it?'

'But, my dear Mrs Srankó, it was raining then, and tomorrow we shall in all probability have splendid weather.'

But it was no use arguing with the good woman, she being a better dialectician than Father János was.

'Raining, was it?' she exclaimed. 'Well, one more reason you should bring it with you tomorrow, your reverence, at least it won't get wet, the precious thing. And, after all, my poor dear husband was worthy of it; he was no worse than Mrs Gongoly. He used to be a judge in his time and did a lot for the Church, too; why, it was he who five years ago sent for those lovely coloured candles we have on the altar; they came all the way from Besztercebánya. And the white altar-cloth my husband's sister embroidered! So you see we have a right to the red thing.'

'But I can't make myself ridiculous by burying someone with an umbrella held over me when the sun is shining. You must give up the idea, Mrs Srankó.'

Thereupon Mrs Srankó burst into tears. What had she done to be put to such shame, and to be refused the right to give her husband all the honours due to the dead, and which were a comfort to the living, too? What would the villagers say of her? They would say: 'Mrs Srankó did not even give her husband a decent funeral, they only threw him into the grave like a beggar.'

'Please do it, your reverence,' she begged tearfully, and kept on wiping her eyes with her handkerchief, until one of the corners which had been tied in a knot came unfastened, and out fell a ten-florin note. Mrs Srankó picked it up, and put it delicately on the table.

'I'll give this over and above the other sum,' she said, 'only let us have all the pomp possible, I beg of you.'

At this moment Widow Adamecz rushed in from the kitchen, flourishing an immense wooden spoon in the air.

'Yes, your reverence, Srankó was a good, pious man; not all the gossip you hear about him is true. And even if it were, it would touch Mrs Gongoly as much as him, may God rest her soul. If the holy umbrella was used at her funeral, it can be used at his, too. If God is angry at its having been used for her, He will only be a little more angry at its being used for him; and if He was not angry then, He won't be angry now either.'

'You ought to be ashamed of yourself, Mrs Adamecz, talking such nonsense. Don't bother me any more with your superstitions. The whole thing is simply ridiculous.'

But the two women were not to be put off.

'We know what we know,' they said, nodding their heads sagely; 'your reverence can't deceive us.'

And they worried him to such an extent that he was obliged at last to give way, and agreed to bring the red umbrella to János Srankó's funeral, but he added as an afterthought: 'That is, of course, if the owner does not come for it before then. For it is certain that someone left it here, and if they come for it, I shall be obliged to give it them.'

'Well,' said Widow Adamecz, 'as far as that goes we can sleep in peace, for the one who brought it only walks on our planet once in a thousand years.'

Nobody appeared to claim the umbrella, and so the next day, though it was a lovely afternoon, and not a cloud was to be seen on the horizon, the young priest opened his umbrella, and followed the coffin to the grave.

Four strong men, Szlávik, Lajkó, and the two burly Magát brothers, carried the bier on which the coffin was placed, and as God willed it, when they passed the smithy, one of the bearers stumbled and fell, which so startled the one walking behind him that he lost his presence of mind, the bier lurched to one side, and the coffin fell to the ground.

It cracked, then the fastenings gave way, and it broke to pieces; first the embroidered winding-sheet was visible, and then the supposed dead man himself, who awoke from the trance he had been in, moved slightly, took a deep breath, and whispered:

'O God, where am I?'

Of course, everyone was as surprised as they could be, and there was plenty of running backwards and forwards to the smithy for blankets, shawls, and pillows, of which they made a bed in a cart that was outside waiting to be repaired. Into this they put the man on whom such a miracle had been worked, and the funeral procession returned as a triumphant one to Srankó's house. He had so far recovered on the way home as to ask for something to eat immediately on his arrival.

They brought him a jug of milk, at which he shook his head. Lajkó offered him a flask of brandy he had taken with him to cheer his drooping spirits. He smiled and accepted it.

This famous incident was the beginning of the umbrella legend which spread and spread beyond the village, beyond the woods, beyond the mountains, embellished and refreshed with newer and newer details as it went.

If a mark or impression were found on a rock, it was said to be the print of St Peter's foot. If a flower of particularly lovely colour were found growing on the meadow, St Peter's stick had touched the spot. Everything went to prove that St Peter had been in Glogova lately. After all, it was no common case.

The umbrella itself shone in the miraculous light of mysticism. Indeed, the only circumstance shrouded in a cloud of mystery was how the umbrella had come to be spread over little Veronica's basket; but that was enough. Superstition seeks darkness, darkness attracts superstition. Those two had shared the spoils, the battered umbrella.

And its fame spread far and wide, as far as the Biela Voda flows; the simple Slovak peasants told the tale sitting round the fire, or in the spinning-room, with various additions and embellishments, according to the liveliness of their imagination. They imagined St Peter opening the gates of Heaven, and coming out with the umbrella in his hand to bring it down to the priest's little sister. The only question they could not settle was how St Peter had got down to the earth. But they thought he must have stood on a cloud which let him gently down and set him on the top of one of the neighbouring hills.

Then they discussed the power the umbrella possessed of raising the dead to life, and so the legend was spread abroad and with it the fame of the parson of Glogova and of his little sister. (What a lucky fellow he who would marry her one day!) And whenever a rich peasant died, even in the villages miles off, Father János was sent for, with the holy red umbrella, to read the burial services. He was also sent for to persons hopelessly sick who wished the umbrella spread over them whilst they confessed their sins. It was impossible that it would not have a good effect; either the sick person would recover, or if he did not do that he would at least be saved.

If a newly married couple wished to do things in a grand way (and they generally do), they were not only married at home by their own priest, but they made a pilgrimage to Glogova in order to join hands once more under the sacred umbrella. And that, to them, was the real ceremony. The bell-ringer held the holy linen-mushroom over their heads, and in return many a piece of silver found its way into his pocket.

And as for the priest, money and presents simply poured in upon him.

At first he fought against all this superstition, but after a while even he began to believe that the red umbrella, which day by day got more faded and shabby, was something out of the common. Had it not appeared on the scene as though in answer to his prayer, and was it not the source of all his good fortune?

'Oh, Lord Jesus!' he had prayed on that memorable morning, 'unless Thou workest a miracle, how am I to bring up the child?'

And lo and behold, the miracle had been worked! Money, food, all the necessaries of life flowed from that ragged old umbrella. Its fame spread to higher circles, too. His Excellency the Bishop of Beszterce heard of it and sent for Father János and the umbrella; and after having examined it and heard the whole story, he crossed his hands on his breast and exclaimed: *'Deus est omnipotens.'* Which was equivalent to saying he believed in it.

A few weeks later he went still further, and sent orders for the umbrella to be kept in the church, instead of in the priest's room.

Upon which Father János answered that in reality the umbrella belonged to his little sister, who was still a minor, so that he had no right to it, nor to give it away. But he was sure, as soon as Veronica was of age, she would make a present of it to the church.

But the umbrella not only brought good fortune to the priest, who soon started a small farm and in a few years built himself a new house and kept a horse and trap, but it made a great difference to Glogova, too. Every summer numbers of ladies came from the small watering-places round about, very often countesses, too (mostly old countesses), in order to say a prayer under the umbrella, and for these an inn was built opposite the priest's house, called the 'Miraculous Umbrella'. In fact, Glogova increased in size and importance from day to day.

In time the villagers began to feel ashamed of the simple wooden belfry, and had a tower built to the church, and hung two bells in it from Besztercebánya. János Srankó had a splendid statue of the Holy Family erected in front of the church, to commemorate his resurrection from the dead. The governess (for a time Father János had a real governess—who wore a hat—for little Veronica) filled the priest's garden with dahlias, fuchsias, and other flowers which the inhabitants of Glogova had never yet seen.

Everything improved and was beautiful (except Widow Adamecz, who got uglier day by day), and the villagers even went so far as to discuss on Sunday afternoons, when people have plenty of time for idle talk, whether they should not build a calvary, like the one they had at Selmecbánya, upon the mountain St Peter had been seen on, in order to make it a place of pilgrimage and attract even more visitors.

PART TWO

The Gregorics Family

- I -

The Tactless Member of the Family

Many years before our story begins there lived in the famous township of Besztercebánya a man of the name of Pál Gregorics who was always called a tactless man, whereas all his life was spent in trying to please others. Pál Gregorics was always chasing Popularity, that charming and coquettish young lady, and, instead of finding it, came face to face with Criticism, that ugly pop-eyed witch.

He was born a full nine months after the day of his father's funeral, an act of tactlessness in itself which gave rise to plenty of gossip, a source of unpleasantness to his mother, who was incidentally a good and honest woman. If he had only arrived a little earlier . . . but after all he could not help it. As far as the other living Gregoricses were concerned, he had better not have been born at all, for, of course, the estates were cut up more than they would otherwise have been.

The child was weak and sickly, and his grown-up brothers always hoped for his death; however, he was tactless enough not to die, but grew up, and when of age took possession of his fortune, most of which he had inherited from his mother who had died during his minority and left him her whole fortune; whereas the children of the first wife only had their share of the father's fortune, which, however, was not to be sneered at either, for old Gregorics had done well in the wine trade. In those days it was easier to get on in that line than it is now, for, in the first place there was wine in that part of the country, and in the second place there were no Jews. In these days, there is much less juice of the grape in the wine-cellars, but plenty of the water of the Garam river.

Nature had blessed Pál Gregorics with a freckly face and red hair which made people quote the old saying, 'Red-haired people are no good.'

So Pál Gregorics made up his mind to prove that it was untrue. All these old sayings are like pots in which generations have been cooking for ages, and Pál Gregorics intended to break one of them. He meant to be as good as a piece of bread, and as soft as butter which allows itself to be spread equally well on white bread or black. As I say, he made up his mind to be a very kindly and amiable person and all he lived for was to be liked by his fellow men.

And he was as good a man as you could wish to see, but what was the good of it? Some evil spirit always seemed to accompany him and induce people to misunderstand his intentions.

The day he came back from Pest, where he had been reading for the bar, he went into a tobacconist's shop and bought some fine Havanas, which at once set all the tongues in Besztercebánya wagging.

'The good-for-nothing fellow smokes sevenpenny cigars, does he? That is a nice way to begin. He'll die in the workhouse. Oh, if his poor dead father could rise from his grave and see him! Why, the old man used to mix dried potato leaves with his tobacco to make it seem more, and poured the dregs of the coffee on it to make it burn slower.'

When it came to Pál Gregorics's ears that he had scandalized the good townsfolk by smoking such costly cigars, he immediately took to short halfpenny ones. But this did not suit people either, and they remarked:

'Really, Pál Gregorics is about the meanest man going; he'll be worse than his father was! What a loathsome miser!'

Gregorics felt very vexed at being called mean, and decided to take the very next opportunity to prove the contrary. The opportunity presented itself in the form of a ball, given in aid of a hospital, and of which the Mayoress of the town was patroness. The programme announced that though the tickets were two florins each any larger sum would be gratefully accepted. So Pál Gregorics gave twenty florins for his two-florin ticket, thinking to himself, 'They shan't say I am mean this time.'

Upon that the members of the committee put their heads together and decided that Pál Gregorics was a tactless fellow. It was the greatest impertinence on his part to outbid the Mayor, and a baron to boot! Baron Radvánszky had given ten florins for his ticket, and Gregorics throws down twenty. Why, it is an insult. The son of a wine merchant! What a century, my God! A flea coughing louder than a lion! What a century! How marvellous a century!

Whatever poor Pál Gregorics did was wrong; if he quarrelled with someone and would not give in, they said he was a brawler; and if he gave in, he was a coward.

Though he had studied law, he did nothing particular at first, only drove to his estate (which he had inherited from his mother), a mile or two out of the town and spent a few hours shooting; or he went for a few days to Vienna, where he had a house, likewise inherited from his mother; that was all he did, to the contempt of the industrious people of Besztercebánya.

'Pál Gregorics,' they said, 'is an idler, he lets the grass grow under his feet for weeks on end. Why are such useless creatures allowed to live?'

Pál heard this, too, and quite agreed with them that he ought to get some work to do and not waste his life as he was doing. Of course, everyone should earn the bread they eat. So he said he would willingly serve his town or country with his brain.

That was enough to set all the tongues wagging again. What? Gregorics wanted work in the town? Was he not ashamed of himself, trying to take the bread out of poor men's mouths when he had plenty of cake for himself? Let him leave the small amount of employment there was in the town to those who really needed it.

Gregorics quite understood the force of this argument and gave up his idea. He now turned his thoughts towards marriage and determined to start a family; after all, that was as good an occupation as any other.

So he began to frequent various houses where there were pretty girls to be met, and where he, being a good match, was well received, but his intriguing stepbrothers, who were always in hopes that the wheezy little man would not live long, did their best to upset his plans with such wily machinations as would provide ample subjects for another story. So Pál Gregorics got so many refusals one after the other that he was soon renowned in the whole neighbourhood.

Later on he could have found many who would have been glad of an offer from him rather than remain an old maid, but they were ashamed to let him see it. After all, how could they marry a man whom so many girls had refused?

On the eve of St Andrew's any amount of lead was melted by the young girls of the town, but not one of them saw in the hardened mass the form of Pál Gregorics. In fact, none of the young girls wanted to marry him. What they looked for was romance, not money. Perhaps some old maid would have jumped at his offer, they are quicker to jump . . . But from young girls to old maids it is not one leap but two: the young married women are in between. Old maids are the last resorts.

Between the young maids and the old maids there is a great difference—they belong to two different worlds. As soon as little Caroline is told that Pál Gregorics spits blood, she is frightened and at his next visit there is only compassion in the fast-beating little heart which yesterday when he first drove up in his coach and four was meant to be filled with quite different sentiments. Poor Pál Gregorics! Spitting blood, the miserable wretch! The horses outside may paw the ground and toss their manes as much as they like, what difference does it make? Pál Gregorics spits blood!

Oh, you silly little Caroline! Of course, Pál Gregorics is an ugly, sickly man, but think how rich he is, and after all, he only spits his own blood. So what is it to you?

Believe me, Caroline—Rosalia, who is a mere ten years older than you, would not be such a silly little goose if she had your chances, for she already is a philosopher, and if she were to be told that Pál Gregorics spat blood she would only think to herself, 'What an interesting man!' And aloud she would say, 'I will nurse him.' And deep down in her mind where she keeps the ideas that cannot be put into words, which, in fact, are hardly even thoughts as yet, only the dregs of selfish sentiments, she would find these words, 'If Gregorics spits blood already, he won't last so very long.'

You silly little girls, you know nothing of life as yet; your mothers have put you into long dresses, but your minds have not grown in proportion. Don't be angry with me for speaking so plainly, but it is my duty to show my readers why Pál Gregorics did not find a wife amongst you. The reason is a simple one. The open rose is not perfectly pure; bees have bathed in its chalice, insects have slept in it. But in the heart of an opening bud, not a speck of dust is to be found.

That is why Pál Gregorics was refused by so many young girls, and by degrees he began to see that they were right (for, as I said before, he was a good, simple man), marriage was not for him, as he spat blood, for, after all, blood is one of the necessaries of life. When he had once made up his mind not to marry, he troubled his head no more about the girls, but turned his attention to the young married women. He had beautiful bouquets sent from Vienna for Mrs Vozáry, and one fine evening he let five hundred nightingales loose in Mrs Muskélyi's garden. He had had the greatest difficulty in getting so many together, but a bird-fancier in Transylvania had undertaken to send them to him. The beautiful young woman, as she was tossing her alabaster body on her pillows, was surprised to hear how delightfully the birds were singing in her garden that night.

To dally with young married women, that is a proper yardstick. Neither a young maid nor an old one can tell what a man is worth —their judgement is coloured by looking at the problem from an angle, but the young women appraise a man from under the Tree of Knowledge; they are no dreamers any longer, nor have they any reason to be impatient; so that their cool appraisal can be relied on. The weight a man pulls with young married women is, it seems, his correct weight.

Well, not to beat about the bush, Gregorics had no success with the young married women either, it being always the wife that turned him out, not the husband, although he would have liked the latter to be furious, not the former. He was beginning to get thoroughly sick of life, when the War of Independence broke out.

But they would not take him for a soldier either; they said he was too small and thin, he would not be able to stand the fatigues of war. However, he wanted to do something at any cost.

The recruiting officer, who was an old friend of his, gave him the following advice:

'I don't mind taking you if you particularly wish to work with us, but you must look out for some occupation with no danger, attached to it. There is plenty of clerical work during a campaign, we'll give you something in the writing business.'

Gregorics was wounded in his pride. He drew himself up like an owl aping a peacock.

'I intend accepting only the most dangerous assignment,' he said. 'Now, which do you consider the most dangerous?'

'Why, that of a spy,' was the answer.

'Then I will be a spy.'

And he kept his word. He dressed himself as one of those vagrants of whom so many were seen at the time, and went from one camp to the other, doing useful service to the Hungarian army. Old soldiers remember and still talk of the little man with the red umbrella, who always managed to pass through the enemy's camp, his gaze as vacant as though he were unable to count up to ten. With his thin, bird-like face, his ragged trousers, his battered top-hat, and his crooked red umbrella, he was seen everywhere. If you once saw him it was not easy to forget him, and there was no one who did not see him, though few guessed at his business. But General Dembinszky of the Hungarian army once said about him: 'The little man with the red umbrella is the devil himself, but he belongs to the sort of good devils.'

In the peaceful time that succeeded the war he returned to Besztercebánya, and became a misanthrope. He never moved out of his ugly, old stone house, and thought no more of making a position for himself, nor of marrying.

And like most old bachelors he fell in love with his cook. His theory now was to simplify matters, to make them as simple as humanly possible. He needed a woman to cook for him and to wait on him, and he needed a woman to love; that means two women in the house. Why should he not simplify matters and make those two women one?

Anna Wibra was a big stout woman, somewhere from the neighbourhood of Detva, where men began above six feet and were strong and straight as the trees of the woods they lived in. She was a rather good-looking woman, and used to sing very prettily when washing up the plates and dishes in the evening. She had such a nice soft voice that her master once called her into his sitting-room, and made her sit down on one of the leather-covered chairs. She had never sat so comfortably in her life before.

'I like your voice, Anna; sing me something here, so that I can hear you better.'

So Anna started a very melancholy sort of Slovak song, 'The Recruit's Letter', in which the soldier complains to the girl he loves of all the hardships of war.

Gregorics was quite softened by the music, and three times he exclaimed: 'What a wonderful throat you've got, Anna Wibra, what a wonderful throat!' And he kept moving nearer and nearer to that wonderful throat till all at once he began to stroke it as if he were only interested in its wonderful construction. This Anna suffered in silence, but when, by accident or design, the stroking hand

- 53 -

went lower, she turned scarlet and jumped up from her chair, pushing him away from her.

'That's not in my contract, sir!' she exclaimed.

Gregorics blushed, too.

'Don't be silly, Anna,' he said in a hoarse voice.

But Anna tossed her head and walked to the door.

'Don't run away, you stupid woman. I shan't eat you.'

But Anna would not listen, and took refuge in her kitchen, from which she was not to be coaxed again that evening.

The next day she gave notice to leave, but her master pacified her by the gift of a golden ring, and a promise never to lay a finger on her again. He told her he could not let her go, for he would never get anyone to cook as well as she did. Anna was pleased with the praise and with the ring, and stayed, on condition that he kept his promise. He did keep it for a time, and then forgot it, and Anna was again on the point of leaving. But Gregorics pacified her this time with a necklace of corals with a golden clasp, like the Baronesses Radvánszky wore at church. The necklace suited that white throat of hers so well that she no longer thought of forbidding her master to touch her. He was rich enough, let him buy her a few pretty things.

In fact, the same afternoon she paid a visit to the old woman who kept a grocer's shop next door, and asked whether it would hurt very much to have her ears pierced. The old woman laughed.

'Oh, you silly creature,' she said, 'you surely don't want to wear ear-rings? Anna, Anna, you have bad thoughts in your head.'

Anna protested and then banged the door behind her, so that the bell fastened to it went on ringing for some time.

Of course, she wanted some ear-rings, why should she not have some? God had given her ears the same as to all those grand ladies in silken frocks she saw at church. And before the day was over she had found out that it would hardly hurt her more than a fleabite to have her ears pierced.

Yes, she wanted to have some ear-rings, and now she did all she could to bring Gregorics into temptation. Such a thing *can* be done, as Eve's every daughter only too well knows. She dressed neatly, wore a flaming red ribbon in her flaxen hair, and discarded the tight, forbidding bodice which concealed her forms for an invitingly low-necked blouse of sheer cambric whose translucent rotundity was a permanent danger to male eyes.

Gregorics may have been artful and wily enough as a spy to outsmart the Russian and Austrian armies put together, but as far as cunning and artfulness went he could not hold a candle to a woman, even to a simple peasant woman of the village of Detva. Next Sunday she went to church with ear-rings in her ears, much to the amusement of the lads and lasses of the town, who had long ago dubbed her 'the Grenadier'.

And in a few weeks' time the whole town was full of gossip about Gregorics and his cook, and all sorts of saucy tales were told, some of them supremely ridiculous. His stepbrothers would not believe it.

'A Gregorics and a servant! Such a thing was never heard of before!'

The neighbours tried to pacify them by saying there was nothing strange in the fact, on the contrary, it was quite natural. Pál Gregorics had never done things correctly all his life. For the rest, it was they who would profit by it seeing that he would never marry and do them out of their inheritance.

How much was true and how much false is not known, but the gossip died away by degrees, only to awaken again some years later, when a small boy was seen playing about with a pet lamb in Pál Gregorics's courtyard. Who was the child? Where did he come from? Gregorics himself was often seen playing with him. And people, who sometimes out of curiosity looked through the keyhole of the great wooden gates, saw Gregorics, with red ribbons tied round his waist for reins, playing at horses with the child, who with a whip in his hand kept shouting, 'Gee-up, Ráró.' And the silly old fellow would kick and stamp and plunge, and even race round the courtyard.

And now he was still less often seen limping through the town in his strange shabby clothes, to which he had become accustomed when he was a spy, and under his arm his red umbrella; he always had it with him, summer or winter, rain or shine, and never left it in the hall when he paid a visit, but took it into the room with him, and kept it constantly in his hand. Sometimes the lady of the house asked if he would not put it down.

'No, no,' he would answer, 'I am so used to having it in my hand that I feel quite lost without it. It is as though one of my ribs were missing, upon my word it is!'

There was a good deal of talk about this umbrella. Why was he so attached to it? It was incomprehensible. Supposing it contained something important? Somebody once said (I think it was István Pazár who had served in the war) that the umbrella contained all sorts of notes, telegrams, and papers written in his spying days, and that they were in the handle of the umbrella, which was hollow. Well, perhaps it was true.

The other members of the Gregorics family looked with little favour on the small boy in the Gregorics household, and never rested till they had looked through all the baptismal registers they could lay hands on. At last, in Privorec, where Pál Gregorics owned a farm, they came upon the entry they wanted, 'György Wibra, illegitimate; mother, Anna Wibra'.

He was a pretty little fellow, so full of life and spirits that everyone took a fancy to him.

- II -

Dubious Signs

Little Gyuri Wibra grew to be a fine lad, strong and broad-chested. Pál Gregorics was always saying:

'Where on earth does he take that chest from?'

He was so narrow-chested himself that he always gazed with admiration at the boy's sturdy frame, and was so taken up in the contemplation of it that he hardly interested himself in the child's studies. And he was a clever boy too. An old pensioned professor, Márton Kupeczky, gave him lessons every day, and was full of his praises.

'There's plenty in him, sir,' he used to say. 'He'll be a great man, sir. What will you bet, sir?'

Gregorics was always delighted, for he loved the boy, though he never showed it. On these occasions he would smile and answer:

'I'll bet you a cigar, and we'll consider I've lost it.'

And then he would offer the old professor, who was very fond of betting and a great chatterbox, one of his choicest cigars.

'I never had such a gifted pupil before,' the old professor used to say. 'I have had to teach very ordinary minds all my life, and have wasted my talents on them. A sad thing to say, sir.' (At this point he allayed the assailing grief with a pinch of snuff.) 'I feel about them like the Mint. You know the tale, sir? What, you have never heard it? Why, the other day a large nugget of gold was lost at the Mint. They searched for it everywhere, but could not find it. Well, after long inquiries it turned out that the gold had been melted by accident with the copper for the pennies. You understand me, sir? I have been pouring my soul into two or three generations of fools, but, thank goodness, I have at last found a worthy recipient for my knowledge. You understand me, sir, don't you?'

But Pál Gregorics needed no spurring on in this case; he had fixed intentions as far as the boy was concerned, and folks were not far wrong when they (mostly in order to vex the other Gregoricses) prophesied the end would be that Gregorics would marry Anna Wibra, and adopt her boy. Kupeczky himself often said:

'Yes, that will be the end of it. Who will bet with me?'

It would have been the end, and the correct way, too, for Gregorics was fond enough of the boy to do a correct thing for once. But two things happened to prevent the carrying out of this plan. First of all Anna fell from a ladder and broke her leg, so that she limped all her life after, and who wants a lame wife?

The second thing was that little Gyuri was taken ill very suddenly. He turned blue in the face and was in convulsions; they thought he would die. Sobbing and shedding all restraint, Gregorics fell on his knees by the side of the bed of the sick child, kissed his face and cold little hands, and asked despairingly:

'What is the matter, my boy? Tell me what hurts you.'

'I don't know, uncle,' moaned the child.

At that moment there was something touchingly human in old Gregorics; with bony fingers dug into his thin red hair he seemed to suffer every pain the child felt, his limbs began to twitch; his heart broke and let its secret fall. He seized hold of the doctor's hand, and his agony pressed these words from him:

'Doctor, he is my son! He is my son, I say! Save him, and I'll give you a basket full of gold.'

The doctor saved him, and got the basketful of money, too, as Gregorics had promised in that hour of danger. (Of course, it was not the doctor who chose the basket; Gregorics had one specially made by the Slovaks of Zólyom for the purpose.)

The doctor cured the boy, but made Gregorics ill, for he instilled suspicion into his mind by swearing that the boy's illness was the result of poison. Nothing could have upset Gregorics as much as this declaration. How could it have happened? Had he eaten any poisonous mushrooms? Gyuri shook his head.

'No, I haven't, uncle-daddy.' (That was how he called Gregorics then. He added the 'daddy', but did not omit the 'uncle'.)

Well, what could he have eaten? The mother racked her brains to find out what could have been the cause. Perhaps this, perhaps that, perhaps the vinegar was bad. (What was it we had for dinner that day?) Or perhaps the copper saucepans had not been quite clean? Gregorics shook his head sorrowfully.

'Don't talk nonsense, Anna,' he said.

Deep down in his heart was a thought which he was afraid to put into words, but which entirely spoiled his life for him and robbed him of sleep and appetite. He had thought of his step-brothers; they had a hand in it, he was sure. A hand stretched out for the inheritance.

There was an end to all his plans for adopting the boy, giving him his own name, and leaving him his fortune. No, no, it would cost Gyuri his life; they would kill him if he stood in their way. But he did not want him to stand in their way.

He trembled for the child, and hardly dared to love him. He started a new line of conduct, a very mad and cruel one, too. He ordered the boy to address him as 'sir' for the future, and forbade him to love him.

'It was only a bit of fun, you know, my allowing you to call me "uncle-daddy". Do you understand?'

Tears stood in the boy's eyes, and seeing them old Gregorics bent down and kissed them away; and his voice was very sad as he said:

'Don't tell anyone I kissed you, or you will be in great danger.'

Precaution now became his mania. He took Kupeczky into his house, and the old professor had to be with the boy day and night, and taste every bit of food he was to eat. If Gyuri went outside the gates, he was first stripped of his velvet suit and patent leather shoes, and dressed in a ragged old suit kept on purpose, and allowed to run barefoot. Let people ask in the streets, 'Who is that little scarecrow?' And let those who knew answer, 'Oh that is the child of Gregorics's cook.'

And in order thoroughly to deceive his relations, he undertook to educate one of his stepsister's boys; took him up to Vienna and put him in the Theresianum, and kept him there in grand style with the sons of counts and barons. To his other nephews and nieces he sent lots of presents, so that the Gregorics family, who had never liked the younger brother, came at last to the conclusion that he was not such a bad fellow after all, only something of a fool.

Little Gyuri himself was sent away to school after a time to Kolozsvár and then to Szeged, as far away as possible, so as to be out of reach of the family. At these times Kupeczky secretly disappeared from the town, too, though he might as well have been accompanied by a drum-and-fife band, for not a soul would have asked where he was going.

Doubtless there was a lot of exaggeration in all this secrecy and precaution, but exaggeration had a large share in Gregorics's character. If he undertook something very difficult he was more adventurous than the devil himself, and once he was seized by fear he saw a thousand spectres loom in every corner. His love for the child and his fear were both exaggerated, but he could not help it.

Whilst the boy was pursuing his studies with success, the little man with the red umbrella was turning his landed property into money. He said he had bought a large estate in Bohemia, and in order to pay for it had been obliged to sell his house in Vienna. Not long after he had built a sugar factory on the estate, upon which he began to look out for a purchaser for his Privorec farm. He soon found one in the person of a rich merchant from Kassa. There was something strange and mysterious in the fact of the little man making so many changes in his old age. One day he had his house in Besztercebánya transferred to Anna Wibra's name. And the little man was livelier and more contented than he had ever been in his life before. He began to pay visits again, interested himself in things and events, chattered and made himself agreeable to everyone, dined with all his relations in turn, throwing out allusions and hints, such as, 'After all, I can't take my money with me into the next world', and so on. He visited all the ladies who had refused him years ago, and very often went off by train, with his red umbrella under his arm, and stayed away for months and weeks at a time. No one troubled about him, everyone said:

'I suppose the old fellow has gone to look after his property in Bohemia.'

He never spoke much about his Bohemian estates, though his stepbrothers were much interested in them. They offered in turns to go there with him, for they had never been in Bohemia; but Gregorics always had an answer ready, and to tell the truth he did not seem to trouble himself much about the whole affair. Which was not to be wondered at, for he had no more possessions in Bohemia than the dirt and dust he brought home in his clothes from Karlsbad, where he spent a summer doing the cure.

The whole story was only trumped up to put his relations off the scent, whereas the truth was that he had turned all he had into money, and deposited it in a bank in order to be able to give it to the boy. Gyuri's inheritance would be a draft on a bank, a bit of paper which no one would see, which he could keep in his waistcoat pocket, and yet be a very rich man. It was well and carefully thought out. So he did not really go to his estates, but simply to the town where Gyuri was studying with his old professor.

Those were his happiest times, the only rays of light in his lonely life; weeks in which he could pet the boy to his heart's content. Gyuri was a favourite at school, always the first in his class, and a model of good behaviour.

The old man used to stay for weeks in Szeged town and enjoy the boy's society. They were often seen walking arm-in-arm on the banks of the Tisza, and when they and Kupeczky talked Slovak together, everyone turned at the sound of the strange language, wondering which of the many it was that had been invented at the Tower of Babel.

When the last lesson was over, Gregorics was waiting at the gate, and the delighted boy would run and join him—though his comrades, who, one would have thought, would have had enough to occupy their thoughts elsewhere, teased him about the old man. They swore he was the devil in person, that he did Gyuri Wibra's exercises for him, and that he had a talisman which caused him to know his lessons well. It was easy to be the first in his class at that rate. There were even some silly enough to declare the old gentleman had a cloven foot, if you could only manage to see him with his boots off. The old red umbrella, too, which he always had with him, they thought must be a talisman, something after the style of Aladdin's lamp. Pista Paracsányi, the best versifier of the form, made up some lines on the red umbrella, which were soon learnt by most of the boys, and spouted on every possible occasion in order to annoy the 'head boy'. But the poet had his reward in the form of a black eye and a bleeding nose, bestowed upon him by Gyuri Wibra, who, however, began to be vexed himself at the sight of the red umbrella which made his 'uncle-daddy' seem ridiculous in the eyes of his schoolfellows, and one day he broached the subject to the old gentleman.

'You might really buy a new umbrella, uncle-daddy.'

'What, you don't like my umbrella?' the old gentleman asked with a sly smile on his face.

'You only get laughed at, and the boys have even made verses about it.'

'Well, my boy, tell your schoolfellows that "all that glitters is not gold", as they may have heard, but tell them, too, that very often things that do not glitter may be gold. You will understand that later on when you are grown up.'

He thought for a bit, idly making holes in the sand with the umbrella, and then added:

'When the umbrella is yours.'

Gyuri made a wry face.

'Thank you, uncle, but I hope you don't mean to give it me on my birthday instead of the pony you promised me.'

And he laughed heartily, upon which the old gentleman began to laugh, too, contentedly stroking his moustache consisting of half a dozen hairs. There was something strange in his laugh, as though he had laughed inwards, to his own soul.

'No, no, you shall have your pony. But I assure you that the umbrella will once belong to you, and you will find it very useful to protect you from the wind and clouds.'

Gyuri thought this great nonsense. Such old gentlemen always attached themselves so to their belongings, and thought such a lot of them. Why, Professor Havrenák had been making his quill pens with the same penknife for the last forty years; he only had a new blade or haft made to it once in a while.

One episode in connection with the umbrella remained fixed in Gyuri's memory ever after, and he gave up arguing about it. One day they rowed out to the 'Yellow', as they call a small island situated just where the Maros and the Tisza meet, and where the fishermen of Szeged cook their far-famed 'fish with paprika'. The younger generation of fishermen know no Latin. Yet this is the only dish that cannot be prepared without at least a smattering of the language, the rest of the ingredients being, of course, sturgeons, sheat-fish, paprika and Tisza water. We read in Márton's famous cookery book that no woman can prepare the dish properly. This may have been an allusion to the ancient rule never lost sight of since fish with paprika had first been made: '*Habet saporem, colorem et adorem.*' (It has taste, colour and flavour.)

Well, as I said, the three of them—Kupeczky, Gregorics and Gyuri—rowed out to the 'Yellow'. As they were landing they struck against a sand-heap, and Gregorics, who was in the act of rising from his seat, stumbled and lost his balance, and in trying to save himself from falling dropped his umbrella into the water, and the current carried it away with it.

'My umbrella, save it!' shouted Gregorics, who had turned as white as a sheet, and in whose eyes they read despair. The two boatmen smiled and the elder one, pushing his pipe from one corner of his mouth to the other, remarked laconically:

'No great loss that, sir; it was only fit to put in the hands of a scarecrow.'

'One hundred florins to the one who brings it back to me,' groaned the old gentleman.

The boatmen, astonished, gazed at one another, then the younger man began to pull off his boots.

'Are you joking, sir, or do you mean it?'

'Here are the hundred florins,' said Gregorics, taking a bank-note from his pocket-book.

The young man, a fine specimen of a Szeged fisherman, turned to Kupeczky.

'Is the old gent mad?' he asked in his lackadaisical way, whilst the umbrella quietly floated down the rippling waters of the lazy Hungarian Nile.

'Oh dear, no,' answered Kupeczky, who, however, was himself surprised at Gregorics's inordinate attachment to the umbrella.

'It's not worth it, *domine spectabilis*,' he added, turning to the old gentleman.

'Quick, quick!' gasped Gregorics.

Another doubt had arisen in the boatman's mind.

'Is the bank-note a real one, sir?' he asked.

'Of course it is. Make haste!'

The man, who had by this time taken off both his boots and his jacket, now sprang into the water like a frog, and began to swim after the umbrella, the old boatman shouting after him:

'You're a fool, Jankó, come back, don't exert yourself for nothing.'

Gregorics, afraid the warning would take effect, flew at the old man and seized hold of his tie.

'Hold your tongue or I'll murder you. Do you want to ruin me?'

'What do you mean? Do you want to throttle me? Leave go of my necktie.'

'Well, let the lad go after my umbrella.'

'After all, what is the hen good for if not to look after the chickens?' muttered the old boatman. 'The current just here is very strong, and he won't be able to reach the umbrella. And what's the good of it, when it will come back of itself when the tide turns in half an hour's time, to the other side of the "Yellow". In half an hour the fishermen will spread their nets, and the gentleman's umbrella will be sure to be caught in them; even if a big fish swallows it we can cut it open.'

And as the old fisherman had said, so it came to pass; the umbrella was caught in one of the fishing-nets, and great was the joy of old Gregorics when he once more held his treasure in his hand. He willingly paid the young fisherman the promised one hundred florins, though it was not really he who had brought the umbrella back; and in addition, he rewarded the fishermen handsomely, who, the next day, spread the tale through the whole town of the old madman who had given one hundred florins for the recovery of an old torn red umbrella. They had never before caught such a big fish in the Tisza.

'Perhaps the handle of the umbrella was of gold?'

'Not a bit of it; it was only of wood.'

'Perhaps the linen was particularly fine?'

'Rubbish! Is there any linen in the world worth one hundred florins? It was plain red linen, and even that was torn and ragged.'

'Then you have not told us the tale properly.'

'I've told you the whole truth.'

Kupeczky remarked to Gyuri:

'I would not mind betting the old gentleman has a tile loose.'

'A strange man, but a good one,' answered Gyuri. 'Who knows what memories are attached to that umbrella!'

-III-

Pál Gregorics's Death and Will

No signification was attached to the above-mentioned incident till years after, when everyone had forgotten all about it, Gyuri included. As for Kupeczky, he could not remember it, for as soon as the news came from Besztercebánya that old Gregorics was dead, he took to his bed and never rose from it again.

'I am dying, Gyuri,' he said to his sobbing pupil, 'I feel it. It was only Gregorics who kept me alive, or rather I kept myself alive for his sake. But now I'm done for. I don't know if he has provided for your future, my poor boy, but it's all over with me, I'm dying, I wouldn't mind betting it.'

And he would have won his bet, too. Gyuri went home for Gregorics's funeral, and a week later the landlady sent word that the old professor was dead, and he was to send money for the funeral.

But what was Kupeczky's death to that of Gregorics? The poor old fellow was quite right to take his departure, for no one wanted him, no one took any notice of him. He slipped quietly into the next world, just as one would expect him to do after an uneventful life; he was here, he went, that's all. But Pál Gregorics played his part in quite a different style.

He was taken ill with cramp on the Thursday in Holy Week, and went to bed in great pain. He sent for some hot bags of barley to put on his stomach. Anna brought in the barley and straightened his pillows. After a time the cramp ceased, but left him very weak, and he fell asleep towards evening. Some hours after he opened his eyes and said:

'Anna, bring me my umbrella and put it here under my pillow. That's it! Now I feel better!'

He turned over and went to sleep again, but soon woke up with a start.

'Anna,' he said, 'I have had a fearful dream. I thought I was a horse, and was being taken to a fair to be sold. My stepbrothers and nephews appeared on the scene and began to bid for me, and I stood trembling there, wondering which of them I was to belong to. My brother Boldizsár pulled open my mouth, examined my teeth, and then said, "He is not worth anything, we could only get five florins for his skin." As he was speaking, up came a man with a scythe. He poked me in the ribs (it hurts me still) and exclaimed, "The horse is mine, I'll buy it." I turned and looked at him, and was horrified to see it was Death himself. "But I will not give the halter with the horse," said my owner. "It does not matter," answered the man with the scythe, "I can get one from the shop round the corner; wait a minute, I'll be back directly." And then I awoke. Oh, it was dreadful!'

His red hair stood on end, and beads of perspiration rolled down his face, which Anna wiped with a handkerchief.

'Nonsense,' she said, 'you must not believe in dreams; they do not come from Heaven, but from indigestion.'

'No, no,' said the sick man, 'I'm going, I feel it. My time will be up when they bring the halter. Don't waste words trying to console me, but bring me pen and paper. I want to send a telegram to the boy; he must come home at once. I'll wait for his arrival, yes, I'll wait till then.'

They brought a table to his bed, and he wrote the following words:

'Come at once, uncle-daddy is dying and wants to give you something—Mother.'

'Send the servant with this at once.'

He was very restless whilst the man was away, and asked three times if he had returned. At length he came back, but with bad news; the telegraph-office was closed for the night.

'Well, it does not matter,' said Anna. 'We will send it in the morning. The master is not really so bad, it is half imagination; but he is so nervous we must not excite him, so go in and tell him the telegram is sent.'

He was quieter after hearing that lie, and began to reckon at what time the boy would arrive, and decided he might be there by the afternoon of the second day.

He slept quietly all night, and got up the next morning very pale and weak, but went about putting things straight and turning out drawers.

'It is unnecessary to send the telegram,' thought Anna to herself. 'He seems nearly himself again, and will be all right in a day or two.'

The whole day he pottered about, and in the afternoon shut himself up in his study and drank a small bottle of old Tokay, and wrote a great deal. Anna only went in once to see if he wanted anything. No, he wanted nothing.

'Have you any pain?'

'My side hurts me, just where the man with the scythe touched me. There is something wrong inside.'

'Does it hurt very much?'

'Yes, very much!'

'Shall I send for a doctor?'

'No.'

In the evening he sent for the notary public, János Sztolarik. He was quite lively when he came, made him sit down, and sent for another bottle of Tokay.

'The February vintage, Anna,' he called after her.

The wine had been left him by his father, the famous wine merchant, and dated from the year when there had been two vintages in Tokay in twelve months, one in February, and one in October. Only kings can drink the like of it. On account of the early onset of the winter in the previous year the 'February vintage' had been left on the stocks till spring, and you can imagine what a flavour those grapes had. There was never anything like it before nor after. Old Gregorics's father used to call it the 'lifesaver' and often said:

'If a man intending to commit suicide were to drink a thimbleful of it beforehand, he would, if unmarried, go and look up a "best man", or, if married, would go and sue for a divorce; but kill himself he would not.'

The two friends drank to each other's health, and Gregorics smacked his lips.

'It's devilish good,' he said. 'Of this my godfather drank the day I was born. That was the beginning and this is to be the end.'

They drank again. The notary liked the wine, too. Then Gregorics produced a sealed sheaf of documents from his pocket.

'In that you'll find my will,' he said. 'I sent for you in order to give it you in safe custody.'

He rubbed his hands and chuckled.

'There will be some surprise in that.'

'Why are you in such a hurry with it? There is plenty of time,' said Mr Sztolarik, taking the packet.

Gregorics smiled.

'I know more about that than you, Mr Sztolarik. But take a drop more, and don't let us talk of death. He is out haggling over the price of the halter. It might be more interesting for you to learn how my father got this wine.'

'I am all ears, Mr Gregorics.'

'Well, he was a very sly customer, and if he couldn't get a thing by fair means, he got it by foul, and I have inherited some of his slyness from him. But mine is not the genuine article; however, that does not matter. In Zemplén there lived a very, very rich man, a count, and an ass into the bargain; at least he was a good-hearted man, and liked to give pleasure to others, thus proving that he *was* an ass. My father used to buy his wine of him, and if they had struck a good bargain, the count used to give him a tiny glass of this nectar. Being an assiduous wine merchant, of course, my father was always worrying him to sell him some of the wine, but the count would not hear of it, and said, "Even the Emperor Franz has not enough money to buy it!" Well, once when they were drinking a small glass of the "life-saver", my father began sighing deeply: "If my poor wife could only drink a thimbleful of this every day for two months, I am sure she would get quite well again." Upon which the count's heart softened and he called up his major-domo and said: "Fill Mr Gregorics's cask with the 'life-saver'." A few days later several visitors arrived at the castle, pretty ladies too, and the count ordered some of the wine to be brought. "There is none left, sir," said the butler. "Why, what has become of it?" asked the count. "Mr Gregorics took it with him, there was not even enough to fill his cask!" It was true, for my father had ordered an enormous cask of Mr Pivák (old Pivák is still alive and remembers the whole story), took the cask in a cart to Zemplén, and, after filling it with the wine, brought it home. Not bad, was it? Drink another glass before you go, Mr Sztolarik.'

When the notary had gone, Gregorics called his man-servant in.

'Go at once to the ironmonger's, Matykó, and buy a large cauldron; then find me two masons and bring them here; but don't speak to a soul about it.'

Now, that was Matykó's weak point; however, if he had not been told to hold his tongue he might have managed to do so later on, when the opportunity for speaking came.

'Off you go, and mind you are back in double quick time!'

Before dark the masons had arrived, and the cauldron, too. Gregorics took the two men into his room and carefully shut the door.

'Can you keep silence?' he asked.

The masons looked at each other surprised, thought it over, and the elder one answered:

'Why, of course we can keep silence, that is the first thing a man does on his arrival in this world.'

'Yes, until he has learnt to talk,' answered Gregorics.

'And even afterwards you can make the trial if it is worth your while,' said the younger man slyly.

'It will be worth your while, for you shall have fifty florins each if you will make a hole in a wall large enough to put this cauldron in, and then close it again so that no one can see where it was put.'

'Is that all?'

'That is all. But besides that you will receive fifty florins each from the owner of this house every year, as long as you keep silence.'

The masons again exchanged glances, and the elder said:

'We will do it. Where is it to be done?'

'I will show you.'

Gregorics took down a rusty key from a nail and went out with the men into the courtyard.

'Now follow me,' he said, and led them through the garden to an orchard in which was a small house built of stone. The most delicious apples grew here, and that had induced old Gregorics to buy the orchard and house from the widow of the clergyman; he had made a present of both to little Gyuri, and it was entered in his name. When the boy was at home he used to study there with Kupeczky, but since he left it had been quite deserted.

Gregorics led the masons to this little house, and showed them the wall in which he wished an opening made large enough to receive the cauldron, and told them when they were ready to come and tell him, as he wished to be present when they walled it in.

By midnight the hole was ready, and the masons came and tapped at the window. Gregorics let them in, and they saw the cauldron in the middle of the room. The top was covered with sawdust, so that they could not see what was in it, but it was so heavy the two masons could hardly carry it. Gregorics followed them step by step, and did not move until they had built up the wall again.

'If you have it whitewashed tomorrow, sir, the devil himself will not find the place the day after.'

'I am quite satisfied with the work,' said Gregorics. 'Here is the promised reward, and now you may go.'

The elder of the two masons was surprised at being let off so easily.

'I've heard and read of this sort of thing, but they did things differently then,' he said disdainfully. 'They used to put the masons' eyes out, so that even they could not find the place again, but, of course, they got a hundred times as much as we do.'

'Ah, that was in the good old times,' sighed the other.

Gregorics troubled his head no more about them, but closed the heavy oaken door of the house and went home to bed.

The next morning the cramp returned, and the agonizing pain was only partially relieved by the amber drops Anna gave him, and the mustard paper she put on his belly. He was frightfully weak, and a dull, ghastly dimness appeared in his eyes. He kept groaning and panting, and only now and then showed interest in what was going on around him.

'Give us a good dinner, Anna,' he said once, 'and make dumplings, the boy likes them.'

And half an hour afterwards:

'Make the dumplings with jam, Anna, the boy likes them best so.' The only thing he would take himself was mineral water. He gulped it down greedily; apparently it did him good, quenching the terrible thirst that was burning his inside. Towards afternoon the cramp was much worse and he began to vomit blood. Anna was frightened and began to cry, and asked if he would not have a doctor or a priest. Gregorics shook his head.

'No, no, I am quite ready to die, everything is in order. I am only waiting for Gyuri. What time is it?'

The church clock just then struck twelve.

'It is time the coach arrived. Go and tell Matykó to wait outside by the gate and carry Gyuri's bag in when he comes.'

Anna wrung her hands in despair. Should she own she had not sent off the telegram? O Lord, he was awaiting him so badly. No, she dare not tell him; she would carry on the deception, and send Matykó out to the gate. But the sick man got more and more restless.

'Anna,' he said, 'take the horn out [an immense horn there hung on the wall suspended by a green cord] and tell Matykó to blow it when the boy arrives, so that I may know at once.'

So Anna took down the horn, and had less courage than ever to own the truth.

The sick man was quieter after that; he was no longer groaning and panting, but listened attentively, raising his head at every sound, and stroking the grip of his umbrella every now and then, as if its presence soothed him.

'Open the window, Anna, or I shan't hear Matykó blow the horn.'

The sunlight streamed in through the open window, and the perfume of acacia blossoms was borne in on the breeze. Gregorics breathed it in deeply, and the sunshine and fragrance stirred up a long-dulled sentiment in the bottom of his heart.

'Put your hand on my forehead, Anna,' he said in a barely audible whisper. 'I want to feel a woman's hand on my body once again.'

He closed his eyes while Anna kept her hands pressed to his temples; he seemed to enjoy the pressure of her fingers on his head. She felt no fever on his forehead, rather it was cold and dry; the skin lacked its natural moistness and seemed to peel off upon the touch.

The sick man sighed.

'Your hand isn't smooth enough, it is too rough, Anna. But the boy's is so soft and warm,' he added as an afterthought.

He smiled faintly, then opened his eyes.

'Did you not hear anything? Listen! Was that the horn?'

'I don't think so. I heard nothing.'

Querulously, Gregorics pointed to the next room.

'That blasted clock is making all that noise,' he said. 'Stop it. Quick, quick!'

An ancient clock was ticking in the next room on the top of a cupboard. It was a beautiful clock Gregorics's father had bought when a Szentiványi had been sold up in Gömör. It was the shape of an ebony vestibule with alabaster pillars and golden handrails, with a heavy pendulum swinging from one wall to the other to the accompaniment of a dull, raspy ticking.

Anna got on a chair and, standing on tiptoe, stopped the clock.

In that moment she heard a sound in the next room, something like a groan, then in a choking voice the muttered words: 'I hear the horn!' then another groan and a thud.

Anna jumped off the chair, and ran into the next room. There all was still; on the bed were large splashes of blood, and Gregorics lay there dead, his face white, his eyes wide open and staring at the ceiling. One hand hung down by his side, the other firmly held the umbrella.

Thus died poor Pál Gregorics, and the news of his death soon spread among his relations and his neighbours. The doctor said he had died of gastric ulcer. He jabbered something—and richly interspersed his speech with Latin words—that the stomach lining got perforated, which caused haemorrhage, and said that if he had been called sooner he might have saved him.

Boldizsár Gregorics was soon on the spot, also his brother Gáspár with all his family.

But Mrs Panyóki (*née* Esmeralda Gregorics), the eldest half-sister of the deceased, was in the country as always in summertime, and on receipt of the news late the same evening, she exclaimed despairingly:

'What a blow, what a blow that he should die in the summer! Here have I been praying all my life for him to die in the winter, and he must needs go and die in the summer. Is there any use in praying nowadays? God, what a blow! Those two thieves will take everything they can lay their hands on.'

She ordered the horses to be harnessed, and drove off as fast as she could, arriving about midnight, by which time the two brothers were in possession of everything, had even taken up their abode in the house, and driven Anna out, in spite of her protests that the house was hers, and she was mistress there.

'Only the four walls are yours, and those you shall have. The rest is ours, and a person who has lived in sin has no business to remain here. So off you go!'

- 74 -

Gáspár was a lawyer, and a man of many words; how was poor Anna to take her stand against him? She could only cry, put on her hat, pack up her box, and move over the road to Matykó's mother. But before she went the two brothers turned her box out to see she took nothing with her to which she had no right: valuables, pass-books or the like.

The funeral took place on the third day. It was not a grand one by any means; no one shed a tear except poor Anna, who did not dare go near the coffin for fear of being sent off by the relations. The boy had not yet arrived from Szeged, and it was better so, for he would probably have been turned out of the courtyard by the two brothers of the dead man. But even though Anna did not walk with the mourners, she was the centre of all eyes, for did not that big house outside the town belong to her now? And when she dropped her handkerchief wet with her tears, did not all the widowed men, one of them even a councillor, rush to pick it up for her? This incident went to prove how much she had risen in people's estimation.

After the funeral, there was a general gathering of all the family at Sztolarik's in order to hear the will read. Well, it was a rather strange one on the whole.

The old gentleman had left 2,000 florins to the Hungarian Academy of Sciences, and 2,000 florins to each of the ladies at whose houses he had visited years before, and to those who had refused to marry him. Nine ladies were mentioned by name, and the legacy had been placed in the hands of the notary public to be paid at once to the legatees.

The relations listened with bated breath, every now and then throwing in a remark, such as, 'Very good. Quite right of him', etc. Only Mrs Panyóki muttered maliciously when the nine ladies' names were read out: 'Dear me, how very strange!'

Boldizsár, who was of the opinion it was not worth while worrying over such trifles (after all, Pál had been slightly mad all his life), said grandly:

'Please continue, Mr Sztolarik.'

The notary answered shortly: 'There is no more!'

Their surprise was great, and there was a general rush to look at the will.

'Impossible!' they all exclaimed at once.

The notary turned his back on them, repeating:

'I tell you, there is not another word!'

'And the rest of his fortune, his estates in Bohemia?'

'There is no mention of them. I can only read what I see written here; you must at least understand that, gentlemen.'

'It is incomprehensible,' groaned Gáspár.

'The curious of it is,' remarked Boldizsár, 'that there is no mention of that cook woman and her brat, though all the world knows what it knows.'

'Yes, of course,' Gáspár joined in, 'there is something fishy here.'

The notary hastened to reassure them.

'It can make no difference to you,' he said. 'Whatever fortune there may be that is not mentioned in the will falls to you in any case.'

'Yes, of course,' said Gáspár, 'and that is only right. But the money? Where is it? There must be any amount of it. I'm afraid some underhand dealing has been done.'

Mrs Panyóki said nothing, only looked suspiciously at her two brothers.

- I V -

The Avaricious Gregoricses

The contents of the will soon became known in the town, and caused quite a little storm in the various patriarchal drawing-rooms with their old-fashioned cherry-wood pianos, over which hung the well-known picture, the 'Sortie of Miklós Zrínyi', and their white embroidered table-cloths on small tables, in the centre of which stood a couple of silver candlesticks, and a huge glass brought from Pöstyén, the famous watering-place, with the image of the local baths engraved on it, the glass holding a bunch of lilac. Yes, in those dear little drawing-rooms there was any amount of gossip going on.

'It was really disgraceful of Gregorics. He had always been tactless, but the idea of compromising honest old ladies, mothers and grandmothers after his death!'

The nine ladies were the talk of the town, their names were in every mouth, and though there were many who blamed Gregorics, there were also some who said:

'After all, who knows what ties there were between them? Gregorics must have been the very devil in his youth.'

And even those who disapproved of Gregorics decided that after all there must have been some friendship between him and the nine ladies at some time or other, or why should he have remembered them in his will, but his behaviour was not gentlemanly in any case, even if they were to believe the worst. In fact, in that case it was even more tactless.

'For such behaviour he ought to be turned out of the club, I mean he ought to have been turned out; in fact, I mean, if he were alive he might be turned out. I assure you, if they write on his gravestone that he was a gentleman, I'll scratch it off with my own penknife.'

These were the words of Mihály Vertány, the town clerk.

The town archivist, and at the same time captain of the firebrigade, a man generally accepted as an expert on affairs of honour, looked at it from a different point of view.

'It is a cowardly trick,' he declared. 'Never mind the women. Women only count until they are thirty-five years of age, but these are dowagers, all the nine of them. A little indiscretion of this kind cannot hurt them. If you breathe on a rusty bit of steel, it leaves no mark. We only remove caterpillars from those trees which have flowers or leaves, or which will bear fruit, but on old, dried-up trees we leave them alone. But it is the husbands Gregorics has offended, for it is a cowardly thing to affront people who cannot demand satisfaction from you. And I think I may affirm with safety that Gregorics is now incapable of giving satisfaction. I blame him for this alone.'

On second thoughts the Gregorics brothers themselves began to sling mud on the nine old flames of the deceased, so that already the next morning István Vozáry (whose wife was one of the nine ladies mentioned in the will) appeared indignantly at the notary's and informed him that as his wife had never had anything to do with that insolent Gregorics, she had no intention of accepting the 2,000 florins. As soon as this news had spread, the eight remaining ladies arrived one after the other at the notary's in order to make known to him their refusal of the legacy, as they also had had nothing to do with Gregorics.

I do not know when Sztolarik had had such a lively time of it as on that day, for it was really amusing to see those wrinkled old dames, toothless and grey-haired, coming blushingly to defend their honour.

But it was even livelier for the Gregorics family, for they thus got back the 20,000 florins mentioned in the will—that is, with the exception of the 2,000 florins left to the Academy of Sciences, for, of course, the Academy accepted the legacy, though it also had had nothing whatsoever to do with Gregorics. But the Academy (the tenth old woman) was not so modest as the other nine.

The joy of the Gregoricses soon turned to bitterness, for they could not manage to find out where the Bohemian estates were. Gáspár went off to Prague, but came back after a fruitless search. They were unable to find any papers referring to the estates; not a bill, not a receipt, not a letter was to be found.

'It is incomprehensible, such a thing never happened before,' Boldizsár said.

'Perhaps that foolish sea Shakespeare conjured to Bohemia causes all this confusion; that may have swallowed the Gregorics estate,' remarked Mr Sztolarik ironically.

They were wild with anger, and threatened Matykó and Anna to have them locked up, if they would not tell them where the estates were in Bohemia; and at length they were brought before the Probate Court and questioned. Matykó at least must know all about it, for he had travelled with his master when he had been to Bohemia.

So Matykó had to own that his master had only pretended to leave for Bohemia, but had in reality always gone to Szeged or to Kolozsvár, where Gyuri had been at school.

Oh! that shifty Pál Gregorics, how he had cheated his relations! Now it was as clear as day what the old rascal had been up to (believe me, the earth will cast out his bones one day!), why he had turned all his possessions into money on the sly; of course, he had given it all to that bastard boy. But had he given it him? How could he have trusted hundreds of thousands to a brat of that age? Then, where had he put it? To whom had he given it? That was the riddle the Gregoricses were trying to solve.

The notary, the last person who had spoken to Gregorics, declared he had not mentioned any money, and Anna swore by Heaven and earth that she and her son had not received a penny from him, and were much embittered at the fact of his leaving them without any provision.

She had not a good word to say for the dead man. He had made the boy unhappy for life, spending so much on him and his education, and then leaving him totally without providing for him; so that the boy, for whom expensive professors had been kept, would now be reduced to giving lessons himself in order to enable him to live, for the house would hardly bring in enough to pay for his keep whilst attending the lectures at the University.

'Well,' said Sztolarik, 'if he had intended the boy to have his money, he could have given it straight into his hands, no one could prevent it.'

This was quite true, and that was the very reason it seemed so strange and inexplicable he had not done so. The house in Vienna had been sold for 180,000 florins, the Privorec estates for 75,000, which made over a quarter of a million florins. Good heavens! Where had he put so much money to? If he had exchanged the paper notes for gold, melted it, and eaten it by spoonfuls ever since, he could not have finished it yet.

But Gregorics had been a careful man, so the money must be in existence somewhere. But where? It was enough to drive one mad. It did not seem likely that Anna or the boy should have the money, nor Sztolarik, who was now Gyuri Wibra's guardian. The brothers Gregorics nevertheless did not reject the possibility, and they engaged spies to keep their eyes on Anna and mark any careless word she might utter. Moreover, they looked up a sharp boy in Pest who was to make friends with Gyuri in order to find out from his conversation and his way of living whether he knew anything of the missing money. For Gyuri had gone to Pest to attend the University lectures and study law.

The boy sent word that Gyuri lived very simply, attended every lecture, lived at the 'Seven Owls', and dined at a cheap eating-house known by the name of the 'First of April'. This little restaurant was mostly frequented by law students. On the daily bill of fare was the picture of a fat man speaking to a very thin man, and underneath the following conversation was printed:

Thin man: 'How well you look, where do you dine?'

Fat man: 'Why, here, at the "First of April".'

Thin man: 'Really? Well, I shall dine there too in the future.'

All the same, the fare was not of the best, and perhaps this conversation was intended to make April Fools of people. For the restaurant-keepers of olden times were frank, and even if they lied, they did it so naively that everyone saw through the lie.

Gáspár Gregorics received regular bulletins on Gyuri's mode of life.

'He eats his breakfast at a cheap coffee-house, attends lectures all the morning, dines at the "First of April", the afternoon he passes at a lawyer's office, copying deeds, and in the evening he buys a little bacon or curd for supper, then goes home and studies till midnight. Everyone likes him, praises him, and he will make his way in the world.'

That avaricious Gáspár Gregorics began to wish the boy had the quarter of a million after all, for he might in a few years' time marry his daughter Minka who was just turning from a burgeon into a bud—she might be about eleven, no more.

It was a silly theory, for if Anna had really laid hands on the money, it could not have gone unnoticed at least as far as the boy was concerned. But Anna had only let the house, and Sztolarik sent Gyuri thirty florins every month out of the rent.

The Gregoricses divided the 18,000 florins, refused by the nine ladies, amongst the three of them, and also the few hundreds obtained by the sale of the dead man's furniture and personal property, but the rest of the money was still missing.

The whole town was discussing the question of its whereabouts, and all sorts of silly tales were set afloat. Some said the old gentleman had sent the money to General Klapka, and that one day Klapka would return with it in the form of guns and bayonets. Others said he had a fairy castle, somewhere away in the woods of Lopata, where he kept a very beautiful lady, and even if he had not been able to eat up his fortune in the form of melted gold, a pretty woman would soon know how to dispose of it.

But what made the most impression on everyone was that an ironmonger appeared at Gáspár's house with a bill for a large cauldron Gregorics had bought the day before his death, but had not paid for.

Gáspár gave a long whistle.

'That cauldron was not among the things we sold,' he said. And he went through the inventory again, but no, the cauldron was not there.

'I am on the right track,' thought Gáspár. 'My worthy brother did not buy the cauldron for nothing. Consequently, what did he buy it for? Why, to put something in it, of course, and that something is what we are looking for!'

Boldizsár was of the same opinion, and positively beamed with delight.

'It is God's finger,' he said. 'Now I believe we shall find the treasure. Pál must have buried the cauldron somewhere, thinking to do us out of our rights; and he would have succeeded if he had not been so stupid as not to pay for the cauldron. But luckily in cases of this kind the wrongdoer generally makes some stupid mistake.'

The ironmonger remembered that it was Matykó who had chosen the cauldron and taken it with him, so Gáspár one day sent for the servant, gave him a good dinner with plenty of wine, and began to question him about Pál's last days, cunningly introducing the incident of the cauldron, the bill for which the ironmonger had just sent him as he said.

'What about this cauldron, Matykó?' he asked. 'Did your master really order it? I can hardly believe it, for what could he have wanted it for? I'm afraid, son, you have been buying things for yourself, in your master's name.'

That was the very way to make Matykó speak, to doubt his honour; and now he let out the whole story in order to clear himself. The day before his death, his master had told him to go and buy a cauldron, and bring it to him, together with two masons. He had gone as he was told, and towards evening had taken the cauldron into his master's bedroom; the masons had arrived at the same time, and had seen the cauldron, so they could bear witness to the fact.

'Well, that's right, Matykó, you're a lucky fellow, for if you have two witnesses, your honour is as intact as ever, and you must consider my words as unspoken. Drink another glass of wine, and don't be offended at my suspicion; after all, it was only a natural conclusion; we could find no traces of the cauldron, and the ironmonger wanted to be paid for it, and said you had taken it away. Where can it have got to?'

'Heaven only knows,' answered Matykó with a shrug.

'Did you never see it again?'

'Never.'

'And what became of the masons? What did they come for?'

'I don't know.'

Gáspár Gregorics looked straight into the lad's face and struck an ironical note again.

'You are like "John Don't-know" in the fairy-tale. He always answered "I don't know" to everything that was asked of him. Of course, you don't know the two witnesses either who could establish your innocence? In that case, my good fellow, you're no better off than you were before.'

'But I do know one of them.'

'What is his name?'

'Oh, I don't know his name.'

'Well, how do you know him, then?'

'He has three hairs at the end of his nose.'

'Rubbish! He may have cut them off since then.'

'I should know him all the same by his face, it is just like an owl's.'

'And where did you pick up the two masons?'

'They were mending the wall of the parish church.'

By degrees Gáspár Gregorics got all particulars out of the man, and now the ground seemed to be burning under his feet, so he went straight into the town to look for the mason with the three hairs on his nose.

It was not difficult to find him, and at the first place he asked about the three hairs—an inn frequented by masons—three voices answered at once:

'That must be András Prepelicza, for sure. It is his moustache that made the mistake of growing on the top of his nose instead of on his lip.'

After that it was mere child's play, for every mason and brick-layer's apprentice knew that Prepelicza was 'building Budapest', as they expressed it. He was working at a large house in Kerepesi Street.

Sparing neither trouble nor pains, Gáspár immediately had the horses harnessed and drove to Pest, not stopping till he reached the capital; and there he set to work to find Prepelicza amongst the Slovak workmen. The mason was just going up on a pulley to the third storey when he found him, and Gáspár shuddered as he thought, 'Supposing the cords were to give way now!'

'Hallo, Prepelicza!' he shouted. 'Wait a bit, I was just looking for you. I want to have a talk with you.'

'All right,' called out the mason, examining the newcomer from above. 'Come up if you want to talk.'

'You come down to me, it is very important.'

'Well, shout it out, I can hear it all right up here.'

'I can't do that, I must speak to you in private at any cost.'

'Good or bad?'

'Very good.'

'Good for me?'

'Yes, good for you.'

'Well, if it is good for me, it can wait till the evening. I shall be down by then, but I want to finish this top window first.'

'Don't argue, but come down at once. You won't be sorry for it.'

'Why, I don't even know who you are.'

'I'll send you word in a minute.'

And with the next pulley he sent Prepelicza up a nice new crisp ten-florin note. The man who took it up got a florin for doing so. After the sight of this novel visiting-card, Prepelicza threw down his hammer and trowel, and with the next pulley returned to his mother earth where miracles have been going on ever since the time of Moses and Christ.

'What can I do for you, sir?'

'Follow me.'

'To the end of the world, sir.'

'We need not go as far as that,' said Gregorics smiling. And they only went as far as 'The Cock', a small public house, where they ordered some wine, after drinking which the wily Gáspár began, smiling blandly:

'Can you speak, Prepelicza?'

The mason began to wonder what was going to happen, and looked long and attentively into the small, steely grey eyes of his new acquaintance, and then said guardedly:

'Even a jay can speak, sir.'

'I am from Besztercebánya.'

'Really? There are very decent people there. I seem to know your face too, sir.'

'You probably mistake me for my half-brother,' said Gáspár slyly. 'You know, the one who had the cauldron put away so secretly.'

'The cauldron!' Prepelicza's mouth was wide open from astonishment. 'Was that your brother? Now I understand where the likeness is, at least . . . I mean . . .' (and he began to scratch his ear doubtfully). 'What cauldron are you speaking of? I can't be expected to remember every pot and pan I have seen in my life.'

Gáspár was prepared for such hitches as this, so was not surprised, and offered the mason a cigar, which he immediately wetted to make it burn slower, then lit it, and began to drum on the table like a man who has just found out that he has something to sell, and has the right purchaser before him. Now he must be as phlegmatic as possible, and the price of the article would rise in proportion.

His heart beat loud and fast, and the white cock framed on the wall above the green table seemed to awake to life before his eyes, and to crow out these words: 'Good afternoon, András Prepelicza!

Cock-a-doodle-doo. You have luck before you! Seize hold of it!'

'What do you say, Prepelicza, you don't remember the cauldron? What do you take me for? Do I look like a fool? But I daresay, in your place I should do the same. This wine is very good, isn't it? What do you say? It tastes of the cask? Why, my good fellow, it can't taste of mortar, can it? Here, waiter, fetch another bottle of wine, and then be off and leave us alone. Well, what were we speaking of? Ah, yes, you said a short time ago that even the jay could speak, and that is quite true, you are a wise man, Prepelicza, and the right man for me, for we shall soon come to terms. Yes, even the jay can speak, but only if they cut its tongue. This is what you meant, isn't it?''

'H'm!' was the answer, and the three hairs on the mason's nose began to move, as though a breath of air had passed through them.

'I know, of course, that they cut the jay's tongue with a knife, but as you are not a bird, Prepelicza . . .'

'No, no,' stammered the man hastily.

'Well, instead of a knife I take these two bank-notes to cut your tongue with.'

And with that he took two hundred-florin bank-notes out of his pocket-book.

The eyes of the mason fixed themselves greedily upon the two tempting pieces of paper, upon the two naked boys printed on them, one holding a sheaf of wheat, the other a book; his eyes nearly dropped out of his head he stared so hard, but then he fought down his greed and said in a dull, hoarse voice:

'The cauldron was heavy, very heavy indeed.'

That was all he could get out, whilst he continued gazing at the two charming cherubs on the paper notes. He had six of his own at home, but none of them was as pretty as these.

'Well, my good man,' said Gregorics surprised, 'still silent?'

'It would be like a stone on my heart if I were to speak,' sighed the mason, 'a very big stone. I don't think I could bear it.'

'Don't talk such nonsense! A stone, indeed! Why, you have had to do with nothing else all your life, you need not cry about having one on your heart! You can't expect me to give you two hundred florins, and then give you a hot roll to carry in your heart. Don't be a fool, man.'

Prepelicza smiled at this, but he put his big red hands behind his back, a sign that he did not intend to touch the money.

'Perhaps you find it too little?'

Not a word did he answer, only pushed his hair up in front, till he looked like a sick cockatoo; then, after a few moments, raised his glass to his lips, and drained it to the dregs, and then put it back on the table so brusquely that it broke.

'It is disgraceful!' he burst out; 'a poor man's honour is only worth two hundred florins, though God created us all equal, and He gave me my honour as well as to the bishop or to the Baron of Radvány. And yet you tax mine at two hundred florins. It's a shame!'

Upon that Gáspár decided to play his trump.

'Very well, Prepelicza, you needn't be so cross. If your honour is so dear, I'll look for cheaper.'

And with that he put back the two bank-notes in his pocket.

'I'll look up your companion, the other mason.'

Then he called the headwaiter in order to pay for the wine, Prepelicza smiled.

'Well, well, can't a poor man give his opinion? Of course you can look up the other man, and he won't be as honest as I, probably.' (Reluctantly, he scratched the back of his neck which was disfigured by an ugly boil.) 'But . . . well, put another fifty to it, and I'll tell you all.'

'Very well. It's a bargain!'

And the mason began to relate the events of that memorable night and how they had carried the cauldron through the courtyard and garden to a small house.

'To the "Lebanon"!' Gáspár hissed voluptuously, and even the back of his head perspired. 'To that boy's house!'

And the mason went on to tell how Gregorics had stood by whilst they had walled in the cauldron, and watched every movement, Gáspár throwing in a question now and then.

'Was it heavy?'

'Very heavy.'

'Did no one see you as you passed through the courtyard?'

'No one; everyone had gone to bed.'

Gáspár was quite excited, and seemed to enjoy every word he heard; his eyes shone, his lungs expanded, his thoughts were occupied with the future, in which he imagined himself a rich man, the owner of untold wealth. He might even buy a baronetcy! Baron Gáspár Gregorics! How well it sounded! And Minka would be a little baroness.

That fool of a Pál had not known how to make proper use of his wealth, so it must have increased immensely, he had been so economical!

'And what did my brother pay you for your work?'

'He gave us each fifty florins.'

'That was quite right of him.'

A weight had fallen from his heart at these words, for he had begun to fear Gregorics had given them some thousands to buy their silence, and that would have been a great pity as it would have diminished the sum he hoped to possess before long. For he had decided to buy 'Lebanon', with its cauldron and its orchard. He would go tomorrow to that boy's guardian and make an offer for it. And he rejoiced inwardly at the trick he was playing his brother and sister.

He returned home as fast as horses could take him, and did not even stop at his own house, but went straight on to Sztolarik's and informed him he would like to buy 'Lebanon'.

This was the name they had given to the orchard and house old Gregorics had bought of the clergyman's widow. The goodman had never delivered a sermon from his pulpit in which he would not make mention of the cedars of Lebanon and when he had bought the small plot, he had tried to grow cedars there at first among the apple-trees; but the gentle soil of Besztercebánya disapproved of it and the sarcastic inhabitants of the town christened the orchard 'Lebanon'.

Mr Sztolarik showed no surprise at the offer.

'So you want to buy "Lebanon"?' he said. 'It is a good orchard, and produces the finest fruit imaginable. This year a well-known hotel-keeper bought all the fruit, and paid an enormous price for it. But what made you think of buying "Lebanon"?'

'I should like to build a house there, a larger house than the present one.'

'H'm! There is always a good deal of bother attached to a purchase of that kind,' said Sztolarik coldly. 'The present owner is a minor, and the Court of Chancery must give permission for the sale to take place. I would rather leave things as they are. When the boy is of age, he may do what he likes, but if I sell it now, he may be sorry for it later on. No, no, Mr Gregorics, I can't agree to it. After all, the house and orchard are a *praetium affectionis* for the boy, he spent his childhood there.'

'But if I offer a good sum for it,' broke in Gáspár nervously.

Sztolarik began to feel curious.

'What do you consider a good sum? What do you think of offering for it?'

'Why, I would give . . .' and here he was overcome by a fit of coughing which made him turn as red as a peony, 'I would give 15,000 florins.'

Well, that was a brilliant offer, thought Sztolarik, for Pál Gregorics had bought it of the clergyman's widow for 5,000 florins. It was only a small bit of ground, and a good way from the market which decreased its value exceedingly. And the house cannot be worth more than 2,000 . . .

'*Utcumque*,' said Sztolarik aloud, 'your offer is not a bad one. But, but . . . Well, I'll tell you what, Mr Gregorics. I'll consider your offer a bit, and I must write to the boy about it, too, and also speak to his mother.'

'But I want to settle it as soon as possible.'

'I'll write about it today.'

Gáspár did not wish to say any more about the matter, for fear of awakening the notary's suspicions, but a day or two afterwards he sent a tiny cask of Tokay wine to him (some Pál Gregorics had left in his cellar, and which they had divided amongst them), with the inquiry as to whether he had any answer from Budapest.

Sztolarik sent back word he expected a letter every minute, and thanked him very much for the wine; he also remarked to the footman who had brought it that he hoped it would go smoothly, but whether he meant the wine, or something else, the footman did not quite understand.

Hardly had the man gone, when the expected letter arrived, containing the news that Gyuri agreed to the sale of the orchard, and Sztolarik was just going to send one of his clerks to Gáspár, when the door opened, and in walked Boldizsár Gregorics, puffing and blowing as an overfattened goose from the haste he had made.

'Pray take a seat, Mr Gregorics. To what do I owe the honour of your visit?'

'I've brought you a lot of money,' gasped Boldizsár, still out of breath.

'We can always do with plenty of that,' said the notary.

'I want to buy that poor little orphan's little bit of property, "Lebanon".' (Boldizsár Gregorics had always been notorious for his honeyed talk.)

'Lebanon?' repeated Sztolarik, surprised. 'What on earth is the matter with them all?' he muttered to himself; then continued out loud: 'Perhaps you want it for your brother?'

'No, no, I want it for myself. It would suit me nicely; the view from there is so lovely, and the fruit-trees are so good.'

'It is really strange, very strange!'

'Why is it strange?' said the other, surprised.

'Because I have already one purchaser in view.'

'Well, we won't let him have it. A relative is always a relative; and I daresay I can offer you more than he.'

'I doubt it,' said the guardian, 'the first offer was 15,000 florins.'

Boldizsár never turned a hair.

'Well, I offer 20,000.'

Not till after he had said it did it occur to him that the orchard was worth much less than 15,000 florins, and he turned impatiently and asked:

'Who is the fool who offers so much?'

'Your brother Gáspár.'

At this name Boldizsár turned deathly pale, and dropped gasping on to a chair. His lips moved, but no sound came from them, and Sztolarik thought he would have a stroke, and rushed out for some water, calling for help as he went; but when he returned with the frightened cook armed with a rolling pin and jug of water, the visitor had recovered and began to excuse himself.

'I felt a bit giddy; I often have attacks like this. I'm getting old, you see. And now to return to our discussion. Yes, I'll give you 20,000 florins for "Lebanon", and pay the money down.'

The lawyer thought a minute, then said:

'We can't manage things so quickly, for we must have the consent of the Court of Chancery. I'll see about it at once.'

And he was as good as his word, for such an advantageous sale of the orchard he had never dared to hope for. But all the time he was wondering why the two Gregoricses were so anxious to have it. There must be some reason for it. Supposing they had struck upon gold there, it was not impossible, for had not the Kings of the House of Árpád first dug after gold in these parts, before they discovered Selmecbánya? He decided to send István Drotler, the retired civil engineer, to have a look at the place, and see if it contained gold or coal. But before he had time to start for the engineer's, Gáspár Gregorics appeared on the scene, to ask if there were any letter from Pest. Sztolarik was in difficulties.

'The letter is here, yes, the letter is here; but something else has happened. Another purchaser has turned up, and offers 20,000 florins for "Lebanon".'

This was evidently a great blow for Gáspár.

'Impossible,' he stammered. 'Is it Boldizsár, by any chance?'

'Yes.'

Gáspár was furious, he began to swear like a trooper, his lips trembling with rage, and waved his stick about, thereby knocking down one of Mrs Sztolarik's flowerpots, in which a rare specimen of hyacinth was just blossoming.

'The wretch!' he hissed. And then he sat staring fixedly in front of him for some time.

How did he get to know of it? was the question he was revolving in his mind. It was very simple. That sly Prepelicza could easily find out from some of the workers who had come from Besztercebánya that Pál Gregorics had more than one brother living, and he decided that if one of them paid him 250 florins for the secret, the other would perhaps be inclined to pay something too. So he got into the train, travelled to Besztercebánya, and looked up Boldizsár. There was nothing surprising in that except, perhaps, the fact that Prepelicza was not such a fool as he looked.

'Oh, the wretch!' Gáspár kept on saying. 'But he shall not have it, I will buy it. I'll give you 25,000 florins for "Lebanon".'

Sztolarik smiled, bowed and rubbed his hands.

'It will belong to the one who gives most for it. If it were mine, I would give it you for the 15,000 florins you offered at first, for I always keep my word. But as it belongs to a minor, and I have his interests at heart, I must do the best I can for him. Now don't you think I am right?'

Gáspár agreed with him, and tried to make him promise to give him the preference.

But what was the good of it? Sztolarik met Boldizsár that evening at the club, and made no secret of the fact that Gáspár had been to see him that morning, and offered him 5,000 florins more for the orchard. But Boldizsár was not surprised, and only answered:

'Well, I will give 30,000.'

And this mad auction went on for days until the attention of the whole town was drawn to it, and people began to think the Gregoricses must have gone mad, or that there must be some important reason for their wishing to have possession of 'Lebanon'.

Gáspár came and offered 32,000 florins, and as soon as Boldizsár heard of it, he came and offered 3,000 florins more; and so on, until people's hair began to stand on end.

'Let them go on as long as they like, let the value of the property increase,' thought the president of the Court of Chancery who deliberately withheld his consent to the sale.

And they did go on, until they reached the sum of 50,000 florins, which was Boldizsár's last offer. And Heaven only knows how long it would have gone on still.

The most surprising of it was that Mr Drotler, the engineer who on Sztolarik's instruction had actually inspected the place, had declared there was nothing of any value to be found there, not even a bit of gold, unless it were perhaps the stoppings of some dead woman's teeth.

'But supposing there is coal there?'

'Not a sign of it.'

'Then what on earth are the Gregoricses thinking of?'

Whatever the reason was, it was certainly to Gyuri's advantage, and his guardian felt it his duty to press his luck to the last drop. The grapes are only thrown into the marc when nothing but the skin and seeds are left; who ever heard of throwing them away as long as there still is some more juice to be had of them.

He intended to wait till Gáspár capped Boldizsár's 50,000 florins with 52,000, and then, close the bargain.

But he had reckoned without his host, for one fine day it suddenly occurred to Gáspár (who was the craftier of the two), it was strange Mrs Panyóki, their sister, showed no signs of taking part in the auction. She evidently knew nothing of the existence of the treasure; Prepelicza had not told her the secret, and had thus proved himself a clever man, for if he had told her too, his part in the play was over. Whereas now, when the two brothers had the cauldron in their possession, they would be obliged to pay him hush-money to hold his tongue.

As Gáspár turned all this over in his mind, he began to find it ridiculous for him and Boldizsár to keep on outbidding each other, thus attracting everyone's attention to them, putting money into the boy's pocket, and awakening Mrs Panyóki's suspicions. And whichever bought 'Lebanon' at last, would certainly not be left to enjoy it unmolested by the other. So he decided it would be wiser and at any rate cheaper if they were to work together, buy the property, knock down the wall, share the contents of the cauldron, and pay Prepelicza a certain sum yearly to hold his tongue.

So one day the brothers came to terms, and Sztolarik was very surprised when the next day the door opened, and in walked Boldizsár, announcing that he had thought things over and come to the conclusion that 'Lebanon' was decidedly not worth 50,000 florins, and he had given up all idea of buying it.

'That does not matter,' said Sztolarik, 'your brother will give us 48,000 for it.'

And he waited impatiently till he had a chance of speaking to Gáspár about it. But that good man calmly answered:

'It was very stupid of me to offer so much for it, but I have got it out of my mind like a bad dream. I am really grateful to you, Mr Sztolarik, for not taking me at my word at once. Why, I can buy a good-sized estate for the money I offered for it.'

The guardian hardly knew what to do next. He was afraid he had made them go back on their bargain, by letting them carry it on so long, and felt sure he would be the laughing-stock of the town, and that Gyuri would reproach him with not looking after his interests properly. So off he rushed to Boldizsár and offered him 'Lebanon' for 45,000 florins; but Boldizsár only laughed, scratching his chin and said:

'Do you take me for a fool?'

Whereupon he went to Gáspár and said:

'Well, you may have "Lebanon" for 40,000 florins.'

Gáspár shook his head and answered:

'I am not quite mad yet.'

And now the auction began again, but this time it went backwards, until at last, with the greatest difficulty, Sztolarik got 15,000 florins out of them. They bought it together, and both signed their names to the deeds.

On the day they received the key of the house from the guardian, they both went there, shut themselves in, and began to pull down the inner wall with the pickaxes they had brought with them under their cloaks. They soon found the cauldron, but what was in it has not become clear to this day, though that was the chief point to be settled in the Gregoricses' lawsuit, which took up the attention of the Besztercebánya law-courts for ten years.

It began in this way. A few months after the purchase of 'Lebanon', Prepelicza appeared on the scene and demanded his share of the treasure discovered in the wall, otherwise he would make known the whole affair to Mrs Panyóki. The brothers got mad with rage at the sight of him.

'You miserable thief!' they cried. 'You were a party to the fraud practised upon us by that good-for-nothing brother of ours, who wanted to rob us in order to benefit his bastard boy. He wanted us to buy that ramshackle shanty of his for good money. That is why you helped him to fill the cauldron with rusty nails and bits of old iron. Now you are here, you may as well have your share.'

With that they each seized hold of a heavy stick, and began to beat Prepelicza till he was black and blue. Off he went to a doctor to have him draw a map of the blue lines criss-crossing his back and then to János Krekics, the pettifogger, who had to write a beautiful long letter to the king in his name, complaining of the behaviour of the two brothers Gregorics towards one of his honourably discharged corporals.

'If the king is not ashamed of it, I am not ashamed of it either, they were two to one!' he said to the lawyer.

His third act of the retribution was to hire a cart (for it was impossible for him to walk in his present state) and drive to Varecska, where Mrs Panyóki spent the summer, and tell her the whole tale from beginning to end.

The result was the lawsuit Panyóki versus Gregorics, which furnished the neighbourhood with gossip for ten years. A whole legion of witnesses had to be examined, and the deeds and papers increased to such an extent that at the end they weighed seventy-three pounds. Mrs Panyóki could only prove the existence of the cauldron, its having been walled in, and its appropriation later on by the two brothers, who, on their part, tried to prove that it contained nothing of value, only a number of rusty nails and odd bits of iron with which the deceased had filled it in order to fool them and rob them. As the dead man had neither protector nor lawyer to defend him, he was at long last made responsible for all.

Indeed, there is every reason to believe that he had devised that cruel trick with the nails and odd bits of iron and that his cunning mind was behind the lawsuit which only ended when it made no difference which side lost or won it, for the seventy-three pounds of paper and the six lawyers had eaten up the whole of the Gregorics and Panyóki fortunes.

By degrees all the members of the family died in poverty, and were forgotten; only Pál Gregorics lived in the memories of the six lawyers, who remarked from time to time: 'That was a man with brains for you!'

But in spite of all researches, the dead man's fortune was still missing, not a trace of it was to be found, no one had inherited it except rumour which did as it liked with it, decreased it, increased it, placed it here or there at pleasure.

PART THREE

Traces

- I -

The Umbrella again

Many years passed, many a raft had since swum down the river Garam, and things had changed very much in Besztercebánya, but the thing that will interest us most of all is the gilt-lettered doorplate on the old Gregorics house, on which is to be read: 'György Wibra, attorney at law'.

Yes, little Gyuri is now a well-known lawyer; people come to him from all sides for advice, and young girls smile at him from their windows as he passes. He is a very handsome young man, and clever. He has youth and health, and his whole life before him, what more can he want? Who knows? He may even sit in Parliament one day.

But the narrow-minded inhabitants of the little town do not look so far ahead; they are at present only occupied with one question, namely, whom will he marry?

Why, Katka Krikovszky would marry him any day, and she is the prettiest girl in town. Then there is Mathilda Hupka, who would receive him with open arms if he came to her with a proposal, though she is very high and mighty. And even Mariska Biky would not refuse him, and she belongs to the nobility, and has 50,000 florins. Girls are very cheap nowadays!

But Gyuri Wibra paid no attention to any of them; he was a serious and retiring young man, and his friends soon saw that he was infinitely above them in every way. As a rule, young men first take their diploma, then start an office and look out for clients.

Their house then begins to grow by degrees until finally it seems so large and empty that the young lawyer feels it must be filled with the cheerful presence of a woman, a blonde or a brunette. This is the way of all young and prosperous lawyers.

But it never occurred to Gyuri to marry. And once when Mrs Krikovszky broached the subject to him and asked when they would hear of his engagement, he answered absently:

'Excuse me, I am not in the habit of marrying.'

It certainly is a bad 'habit', but one that does not seem inclined to go out of fashion. For thousands of years people have been marrying, repenting of it, and considering it madness to have done so, but they never get over the madness, and marriage is as fashionable as ever. As long as pretty young girls are growing up, they are always growing up for someone.

Gyuri's business was a brilliant success from the beginning; fortune smiled on him from every side, but he received it with a tolerably sour face. He worked, but only from habit, just the same as he washed himself and brushed his hair every day. His mind was elsewhere; but where? His friends thought they knew, and often asked him:

'Why don't you marry, old fellow?'

'Because I am not rich enough.'

'Why, that is the very reason you should marry. Your wife will bring the money with her.'

(That is the usual opinion of young lawyers.)

Gyuri shook his head, a handsome, manly head, with an oval face and melancholy black eyes.

'That is not true. It is the money that brings the wife!'

What sort of a wife had he set his heart on? His friends decided he must be chasing very high game. Perhaps he wanted a baroness, or even a countess? He was like the Virginia creeper they said, which first climbs very high and then blossoms. But if he were to marry, he could be successful later on all the same. Look at the French beans; they climb and blossom at the same time.

But this was all empty talk. There was nothing whatever to prevent Gyuri getting on in his profession; nothing troubled him, neither a pretty girl's face, nor a wish for rank and riches, only the unhappy legend of the lost wealth disturbed him. For to others it was a legend, but to him it was almost truth, which danced before his eyes like a jack-o'-lantern; he could neither grasp it nor leave it alone. It ran after him in a queer, inexplicable way, persistently and excitingly; cropping up before him from all sides, pursuing him in his dreams and in his waking hours; a voice heard from the walls and from the cobble-stones: 'You are a millionaire, man!'

When he wrote out miserable little bills for ten or fifteen florins, these words seemed to dance before him on the paper:

'Lay down your pen, Gyuri Wibra, you have treasures enough already, Heaven only knows how much. Your father saved it up for you, for he was your father, so you have a right to it. You are a rich man, Gyuri, and not a poor lawyer. Throw away those deeds and look for your treasure. Where are you to look for it? Why, that is just the question that drives one mad. Perhaps sometimes, when you are tired out, and throw yourself down on the ground to rest, it may be just beneath you, it is, perhaps, just beginning to get warm under your hand when you take it away to do something else, and it may be you will never find it at all. And what a life you could lead, what a lot you could do with the money. You could drive a four-in-hand, drink champagne, keep a lot of servants. A new world, a new life would be open to you. The noise of your steps would turn the silver keys in crested doors. And to possess all this you only need a little luck; a flash of the brain; but as you have none at present, take up your pen again, my friend, and go on writing out deeds and bills, and squeezing a few florins out of the poor Slovak defendants.'

It was a great pity he had heard anything about the missing

treasure. He felt it himself, and often said he wished he knew nothing about it, and would be very glad if something were to happen which would go to prove that the treasure did not really exist; for instance, if someone would remark:

'Oh, yes, I met old Gregorics once in Monte Carlo; he was losing his money as fast as he could.'

But no such thing happened; on the contrary, new witnesses were always turning up to assure him: 'Old Gregorics must certainly have left an immense fortune, which he intended you to have. Don't you really know anything about it?'

No, he knew nothing at all about it, but his thoughts were always running on the subject, spoiling all his pleasure in life. The promising youth had really become only half a man, for he had two separate and distinct persons in him. Sometimes he entirely gave himself up to the idea that he was the child of a servant, and an illegitimate one at that, and began to feel he had attained to a really good position by means of his own work, his own personality, and was happy and contented in this thought. But only a word was needed, a thought, to make the lawyer a totally different man. He was now the son of rich old Pál Gregorics, living in abject poverty until he found and took possession of his inheritance. And from time to time he suffered all the pains of Tantalus, and left his office to look after itself for weeks on end, whilst he went to Vienna to look up some of his father's old acquaintances.

The rich carriage-builder, who had bought Gregorics's house in Vienna, did give him some valuable information.

'Your father,' he said, 'once told me when I paid him for the house that he should put the money in some bank, and asked me which would be the best and safest way to set to work about it.' Gyuri wandered then from one bank to another, but without success. Thoroughly worn out, he returned to Besztercebánya with the full intention of not thinking any more about the subject.

'I am not going on making a fool of myself,' he thought. 'I won't let the Golden Calf go on lowing in my ears for ever, and eat up all I possess. I will not take another step in the affair, and shall imagine I dreamed it all.'

But it was easier said than done. You can throw ashes on a smouldering fire—it will put it out, but not prevent it smoking, and the first gush of wind will kindle it afresh.

Sometimes one friend referred to it, sometimes another. His mother, who now walked on crutches, often spoke of the good old times, sitting in her arm-chair by the fire. And at length she owned that old Gregorics had wanted to telegraph for Gyuri on his death-bed.

'He seemed as though he could not die till he had seen you,' she said. 'But it was my fault you came too late.'

'And why did he so much want to see me?'

'He said he wanted to give you something.'

A light broke in upon Gyuri's brain. The mist was clearing up here and there. The Vienna carriage-builder had given him to understand that his father's fortune was represented by a receipt for money placed in a bank, and from the information his mother now gave him he concluded that the old gentleman had intended giving him the receipt before his death. So he must always have kept it by him. But what had become of it? In which bank was the money deposited? Could he, knowing what he did, give up the idea of finding it?

No, no, it was impossible! It could not be lost without a trace! Why, a grain of wheat, if dropped in a ditch, or anywhere else, would sprout and re-appear in time, however unexpectedly. And in a case of this kind, a chance word, a sign, could throw light on the mystery.

He had not long to wait. One day, the dying mayor of the town, Tamás Krikovszky, sent for him to make his will. Several people, holding high positions in the town, were assembled in the room. There lay the mayor, pale and weak, but he still seemed to retain some of the majesty of his office, in the manner in which he took leave of his inferiors in office, recommending the welfare of the town to them, and then, taking from under his pillow the official seal, he put it into their hand, saying:

'For twenty years I have sealed the truth with it!'

Then he dictated his will to Gyuri, and whilst doing so, referred now and then to various incidents in his life, and particularly to the revolution of 1848.

'Dear me, what times those were,' he said once, addressing himself to Gyuri. 'Your father had a red umbrella, with a hollow handle, in which he used to carry valuable papers from one camp to another, in the days when he was a spy.'

'What!' stammered Gyuri. 'The red umbrella?' and his eyes shone.

Like a flash of lightning, a thought had entered his head. The receipt was in that umbrella! His blood began to course madly in his veins, and beads of perspiration gathered on his brow as the certitude of the truth of his suspicion grew upon him. Yes, there it was, he was sure of it; and all at once he remembered the incident at Szeged, how Gregorics had let his umbrella fall in the water, his anxiety, and offer of a large reward for its discovery. Then again, the old gentleman's words rang in his ear:

'The umbrella will once belong to you, and you will find it very useful to protect you from the wind and clouds.' The words resounded so fresh and clear in his ear as though they came right then from the other world.

The bystanders could not imagine why Gyuri seemed so much put about by the mayor's death; in their opinion it was quite right of the old man to take his departure, he had dragged on with his gouty old leg quite long enough, and should now make room for younger men; he had not lived his life for nothing, for were they not going to have his portrait painted and hung in the Town Hall, a grand ending to his life? If he lived for another ten years, he could have no greater honour done him, and his portrait would only be uglier than now.

They were even more surprised at the strange question which Gyuri, in spite of the solemnity of the occasion, put to the dying man.

'And was the hole big, sir?'

'What hole?' asked the mayor, who had already forgotten the subject.

'The hole in the handle of the umbrella.'

There was mild surprise in the glassy eyes when the old man replied, catching for his breath:

'I really don't know, I never asked your father.'

He closed his eyes, and in a weak voice added, with that phlegm which only a Hungarian displays on his death-bed:

'But if you wait a bit, I'll ask him.'

And he probably kept his promise, for half an hour later a black flag was flying from the roof of the Town Hall, and the bells of the Roman Catholic churches were tolling.

Gyuri Wibra had hurried home, nervous and excited, and was now marching up and down his office, his heart beating wildly with joy.

'I have the treasure at last!' he kept on repeating to himself, 'at least, I should have it if I had the umbrella. But where is it?' He could neither eat, nor drink, nor sleep till he had settled it. He questioned his mother on the subject, and she did her best to answer him, but could only repeat:

'How am I to remember that, my dear boy, after so a long time? And what do you want that ragged umbrella for?'

Gyuri sighed.

'If I have to dig it out of the ground with my ten fingers, I will do it.'

'Perhaps Matykó will remember something about it?'

Matykó was soon found; he sat smoking his pipe in the ante-room of the office, for he was now Gyuri's servant. But he also said he had forgotten far more important things than that in all these years; but this much he did remember—that the dead man had kept the umbrella near him till the hour of his death.

'Heaven only knows,' he added, 'why he took such care of the ragged old thing.'

(Not only Heaven knew the reason now, but Gyuri, too!)

He got more information from Mrs Bothár, the old widow who kept the grocer's shop in old Gregorics's house, she had been in the house when he died, and had helped to lay him out. She swore by Heaven and earth that the umbrella had been tightly clutched in the dead man's hand and they had had the greatest difficulty in freeing it from his grasp, and put the holy crucifix there instead.

The lawyer turned away to conceal the tears these details brought to his eyes.

'Yes,' said Mrs Bothár, 'the umbrella was certainly in his hand, may I never move from this spot if it is not true.'

'That's not important,' muttered Gyuri; 'we want to know where it is now.'

'I suppose it was sold with the rest of the things.'

That seemed very likely, so Gyuri went and looked up the list of things that had been sold at the auction. All sorts of things were mentioned—tables, chairs, cupboards, coats, etc.—but there was no mention of an umbrella. He read it over ten times, but it was of no use, he could find no mention of it, unless the following could be considered as such.

'Various useless objects, bought for two florins, by the white Jew.'

Perhaps the umbrella was one of those useless objects, and had been bought by the 'white Jew'. Well, the first thing was to find the 'white Jew'. But who was he? For in those good old days there were not many Jews in the mining towns. There were perhaps one or two in each town, so it was easy to find them; for one was called 'blond', another 'black', yet another 'red', or—if his hair had turned grey—'white', and by means of these four colours the townsfolk were able to distinguish any Jew who lived in their town. But now there were some hundred Jewish families, and Heaven had not increased the shades of their hair to such an extent that each family could be distinguished in the old way.

For all that it was not difficult to find out about the old Jew, and Gyuri soon knew that he was called Jónás Müncz, and it was very likely he had bought the things, for all the old coats and vests of the town found their way into his tiny shop in Wheat Street, before starting on the second chapter of their earthly existence.

Many people remember the little shop in which top-boots, cloaks, and dresses hung on nails, and the following announcement was written with charcoal on the door:

'Only the lilies of the field can dress themselves cheaper than you can in this shop!'

(That was quite true, only with this difference that the lilies of the field were more becomingly dressed than Müncz's customers.)

In spite of all this information Gyuri was by no means satisfied, so he walked across the road to his old guardian's to see if he could find out anything more on the subject from him, for he had been notary public in the town for many years, and must know everyone.

The young man told Sztolarik the whole story, openly and frankly, adding that the receipt for the money, which was probably deposited in some foreign bank, was all but found, for it was most certainly in the handle of the red umbrella, and that had in all probability been bought by an old Jew of the name of Jónás Müncz. All of this Gyuri poured out quickly and breathlessly into the ears of his old guardian.

'That much I know. Now, what am I to do next?'

'It is a great deal, much more than I ever hoped for. You must continue the search.'

'But where am I to search? We don't yet know where Müncz is, and even if we had him, who knows on which dust-heap the umbrella has rotted since then?'

'All the same, you must not lose the thread.'

'Did you know Jónás Müncz?'

'Oh, yes; he was a very honest Jew, that is why he never got rich. He often came to me; I can see him now, with his head bald at the back, and a fringe of white hair round it. 'Pon my word!'— and here the lawyer skipped like a young lamb—'the last time I saw him, he had Pál Gregorics's umbrella in his hand; I can swear to it, and I remember I joked him about it. "It seems to me, Jónás," I said, "that you wander about the next world, too, to buy ole clo', and bought that umbrella there of Pál Gregorics." At which he smiled, and said he had not gone as far as that yet, for he only kept to the two counties of Zólyom and Hont, and had divided the neighbouring counties among his sons; Móricz had Trencsén and Nyitra, Számi had Szepes and Liptó, and the youngest, Kóbi, had only last week been give Bars, but they none of them intended to go into the next world until they were obliged to.'

Gyuri's eyes shone with delight.

'Bravo, Mr Sztolarik!' he exclaimed, 'only the gods had such memories as you have.'

'You are a lucky fellow, Gyuri. I have an impression we are on the right track at last, and that you will find the money."

'I begin to think so, too,' answered Gyuri who was in turns optimist or pessimist, as the occasion presented itself.

'But what can have become of old Müncz?'

'We Christians have a legend about the Jews which says that on the Long Day every year a Jew disappears from the earth and is never seen again. Old Jónás disappeared thus fourteen years ago (you may be sure none of the Rothschilds will disappear in that way). His wife and children waited for him in vain, Jónás never returned. So his sons set out to look for him, and it turned out the old fellow had got soft-headed, and had taken to wandering about in the Slovak villages, where the sons now and then heard of him from people who had seen him; and then one day, they found his dead body in the Garam.'

The young lawyer's face was clouded again.

'Why, in that case the umbrella will be in the Garam too, probably.'

'Perhaps not,' was the answer. 'He may have left it at home, and if so, it will still be amongst the old rags and bones of the Müncz's, for I am sure no one would ever buy it. Try your luck, my boy! If I were you, I would get into a carriage, and drive and drive until . . .'

'But where am I to drive to?'

'Yes, of course, of course . . .'

Then, after a minute's thought:

'Müncz's sons have gone out into the world, and the boxes of matches with which they started have probably become houses since then. But I'll tell you what; go to Bábaszék, their mother lives there.'

'Whereabouts is Bábaszék?'

'Quite near to Zólyom, amongst the mountains. There is a

saying that all the sheep there were frozen to death once, in the dog-days.'

'And are you sure Mrs Müncz lives there?'

'Quite sure. A few years ago they came and fetched her away to be the "Jewess of Bábaszék".'

-II-

Our Rosalia

Yes, they had taken old Mrs Müncz to Bábaszék to be their 'Jew', with forty florins salary, for they had no Jew there, and had to find one at any cost.

As a matter of fact, Bábaszék was just one of those Lilliputian townlets which had nothing more on the rest of the poor highland villages than the fact that they called their judges 'mayors', and on one day in the year a few miserable horses, cows, and pigs were driven in from the neighbouring farms and villages, and Sámuel Plokár, the baker from Zólyom, put up a tent in which he sold gingerbread in the shape of hearts, of soldiers, of cradles, all of which was soon bought up by the young men and fathers of families and taken home to sweethearts or children, as the case might be. In one word, there was a fair at Bábaszék. And for centuries every inhabitant has divided the year into two parts, and remembered the events of the world according as they took place so many weeks or months before the fair, or again after it, as, for instance, the death of Ferencz Deák which happened to fall on the second day after the fair at Bábaszék.

And the reason for all this was that the old kings of Hungary, who lived during the hunting season in the castles of Zólyom and Végles, instead of making grants to the inhabitants, raised the villages to the position of towns.

Well, of course it was a privilege, for in a town everything seems grander than in a village, and is worth a good deal more, even man himself. You are a burgher, not a mere villager, as a member of the council you are called a 'senator', the little straw-thatched house in which questions of moment are discussed is called the Town Hall, and the village crier gives way to the 'hajdú' (town servant) who must even know how to beat a drum—for the town has a drum of its own—the richer ones even have a small fire-engine. After all, position is position, and one must do all one can to keep it up. The more so, when the rumour is going about that before the year is out, most of the small towns with less than a thousand inhabitants are to be deprived of their title. A mad race starts. Being intent on showing off their vitality, they all begin to ride the high horse though their oats won't feed a colt. It will come to no good, you will see . . .

The noble town of Zólyom takes it out of Tótpelsőc.

'That's not a town,' says the former of the latter; 'why, they have not even a chemist's there!' (Well, after all, not every village or town can be as big as Besztercebánya or London!)

Pelsőc on its part will not leave poor little Bábaszék alone.

'That is no town,' they say. 'They have not even a single Jew there. And mark, son, if no Jews settle in a town, it cannot be considered as such; it has, in fact, no future.'

And Bábaszék vilifies those even smaller than itself. But it is not my intention now to write about the squabbles of a string of small towns, I only want to tell you how the leaders of Bábaszék, drawing the lesson of the mud-slingers' vilifications as the bee will draw honey from a poisonous flower, came to enter into negotiations with old Mrs Müncz trying to induce her to move over to Bábaszék.

Well, they sent word to her in Besztercebánya, to come and take possession of the little shop just opposite the market-place near the smithy, where all who travelled through the town must pass. They explained that the commodities most in demand were soap, whips, reddle, washing-blue, scrubbing-brushes, curry-combs, nails, awls, salt, cart-grease, saffron, ginger, cinnamon, lin-seed oil; in fact, all those articles which did not grow in the neighbourhood, or were not manufactured there, though, indeed, there might be some more such besides those listed above.

So that is how Mrs Müncz came to live in Bábaszék, where she was received with great honours, and made as comfortable as pos-sible. It is a wonder they did not bring her into the town in triumph on their shoulders, which would have been no joke, for she weighed at least two hundredweight.

Some of the townsfolk were very discontented that the mayor had only brought a Jewess into the town, and not a Jew, for it would sound grander if they could say: 'Our Jew said this, or our Móricz or Tóbiás did that,' than if they had said: 'Our Rosalia says this, that, or the other,' it sounds so very mild. They would have rather had a Jew with a long beard, and hooked nose, and red hair, if possible; that would have been the real thing!

But Mr Konopka, the cleverest senator in the town, who had made the contract with Mrs Müncz, and who had even gone himself to fetch her and her luggage from Besztercebánya with two large carts, the horses of which had flower and rosettes on, coldly repudiated these aspersions on their Jewess, with an argument which struck as heavily as the stones in David's sling.

'Don't be so foolish,' he said. 'If a woman was once king in Hungary, why should not a Jewess fill the place of Jew in Bába-szék?'

Of course, they soon saw the truth of this, and ceased grum-bling; and they were in time quite reconciled to their Jewess, for every year, on the Feast of Tabernacles, all Mrs Müncz's sons, seven in number, came to see their mother from all parts of the world, and walked about the market-place in their best clothes, laced boots, and top hats. The townsfolk were glad enough then, their hearts swelled with pride as they gazed at the seven Jews, and some of them would exclaim:

'Well, if this isn't a town, I can't tell a midge from a bat!'

'You won't see as many Jews as that in Pelsőc in ten years,' answered another, complacently stroking his belly.

Old Mrs Müncz feasted her eyes on her sons when she sat, as she usually did, in the doorway of her shop, her knitting in her hands, her copper-framed spectacles on her nose (those spectacles lent Bábaszék an additional urban charm). She was a kindly, pleasant-looking old woman in her snow-white frilled cap, and seemed to suit her surroundings, the whitewashed walls of the neighbouring houses, the important-looking Town Hall, and no one could pass her without raising their hat, just as they did before the statue of St John Nepomuk. (She and that statue were, in fact, the only two things worth seeing in Bábaszék.)

Everyone felt that the rotund little gammer would have her share in the progress of the town.

'Good morning, young woman. How are you?'

'Very well, thank you, my child.'

'How is business, young woman?'

'Thank you, my child, getting on very well.'

They were all glad, oh, so glad, that the 'young woman' was so healthy and strong, and that she got richer day by day; they boasted of it wherever they went on their creaking carts.

'Our Rosalia is getting on well. Feathering her nest she is, our Rosalia. But, of course, it is easy to get on in Bábaszék. Bábaszék is a virgin gold-mine . . . Bábaszék is the very place to live in.'

They really made things very comfortable for Rosalia. She was over seventy, but they still called her 'mlada pani' (young woman). And this is not altogether illogical. As the king has grabbed all vain titles and reserves to himself the right of conferring them, so the people (feeling themselves likewise sovereign) have adopted the plan of conferring the 'title of youth', and make use of it when and where they like.

Well, as I said before, they took great care of Rosalia, and when a few years after her arrival there she decided to build a stone house, everyone who owned a cart placed it at her disposal for the carting of stones, sand, wood, etc.; the bricklayers gave a day's work without wages; only one or two of the lazier ones did not join the rest on that day, but were sent to Coventry for it.

'Good-for-nothing fellows,' people said, 'they have no respect for anyone, neither for God, nor priest, nor Jew!'

Their respect went so far as to make them (at the mayor's instigation) set apart two pieces of ground, one for a (future) synagogue, and one for a Jewish burial-ground (for the Jewess they had in the town).

But what did that matter? They had the future before them, and who could tell what it held for them? And it was so nice to be able to weave into your conversation with strangers such meaningful phrases as, 'just a stone's throw from the Jewish burial-ground at Bábaszék', or 'near to the foundation of the synagogue at Bábaszék', and the like.

And the inhabitants of the villages and townlets round about would say when the good folks turned their backs: 'Poor things! Their brains have been turned with the joy of having a Jew in their town!'

- III -

The Traces Lead to Glogova

One fine spring afternoon, a light sort of dogcart stopped before Mrs Müncz's shop, and a young man sprang out of it; nobody else than Gyuri Wibra, of course.

Rosalia, who was just standing at her door, speaking to Mr Mravucsán, the mayor, and Mr Galba, one of the senators, immediately turned to the lissom young man with the question:

'What can I do for you, sir?'

'Are you Mrs Müncz?'

'Yes, sir.'

'I want to buy an umbrella.'

The two gentlemen, surprised, looked up at the cloudless sky.

'What the devil does he want to buy an umbrella for?' muttered Mravucsán to himself.

Then added aloud:

'Where are you from, sir?'

'From Besztercebánya.'

Mravucsán was even more surprised, his chest swelling with

pride. Fancy anyone coming all the way from Besztercebánya to Bábaszék to buy an umbrella! How proud he was it had happened under his mayorship! He nudged Galba:

'Do you hear?' he said.

'This is only a small village shop, sir,' answered Rosalia. 'We don't keep umbrellas.'

'Pity enough!' muttered Mravucsán, biting savagely at his waxed moustache.

'But I heard,' the stranger went on, 'that you had second-hand umbrellas to sell.'

Second-hand umbrellas! Well, what next! Mravucsán, who was asthmatic, began to breathe heavily, and was just going to say something disparaging to the stranger, when some runaway horses attracted his attention. People were fleeing in all directions for dear life; the apprentices at the smith's across the street stopped hammering; shouting and laughing they ran towards the cook's stall whose counter laden with the choicest bits of roast had been knocked over by the stampeding horses. The appetizing joints of pork rolled about in the dust, tickling with their delicious flavour the palates of the hungry lads. The market-women shrieked and moaned, the graver ones took off their bluish aprons, waving them to shy off the horses, and as luck would have it they managed to set them against the bootmakers' stalls. A pandemonium broke out. One of the smith's lads picked up a goodish slice of pork, the market-women rushed after him, whereupon his mate, in a mad attempt to save him, grabbed up a red-hot rod of iron from below the bellows and shook it so at the pursuers' heads that it gave off a shower of sizzling sparks.

In the meantime the two horses were rushing across the market-place, smashing the wares of the Kolpach potter to pieces and dragging the ruins of a handsome phaeton along with them.

'That will never be fit for use again,' said the smith phlegmatically, as he stood looking on, his hands folded under his leather apron.

The phaeton had probably been dashed against a wall, for the left side was smashed to bits, the shaft was broken, one of the wheels had been left somewhere on the road, and the reins were dragging on the ground between the two horses. It was a marvellous sight to watch the infuriated animals which, with manes sagging, mouths foaming, nostrils fuming seemed to be floating in mid-air as if driven by the delirious joy of newly found freedom.

'Beautiful beasts they are,' said Galba.

'They belong to the priest of Glogova,' answered Mravucsán. 'I'm afraid someone may have been thrown out of the carriage; let us go and see.'

During this time the number of customers in Mrs Müncz's shop had increased, and as they had to be attended to, she first turned to the stranger before serving them, and said:

'There are a lot of old umbrellas somewhere on the loft, but they would not do for a fine gentleman like you.'

'I should like to look at them all the same.'

Mrs Müncz had her hand on the door to let her customers in, and only answered without turning round:

'I can assure you, you would not take them in your hand.'

But the young man was not to be put off so easily, he followed her into the shop and waited till the customers were all served, then remarked again that he would like to see the umbrellas.

'But, my good sir, don't bother me about the umbrellas. I tell you they would be of no use to you. They are some that were left from the time of my poor husband; he knew how to mend umbrellas, and most of these are broken and torn, and they certainly will not have improved, lying on the dusty loft so long. Besides, I cannot show them to you, for my son is at the fair, the servant has a bad foot and cannot move, and when there is a fair my shop is always full, so I cannot leave it to go with you.'

The young lawyer took a five-florin note out of his pocket.

'I don't want you to do it for nothing, Mrs Müncz, but I must see the umbrellas at any price. So let me go up alone to the loft, and please take this in return for your kindness.'

Mrs Müncz did not take the money, and her small black eyes examined the young man suspiciously.

'Now I shall certainly not show you the umbrellas.'

'And why not?'

'My poor dead husband used to say: "Rosalia, never do anything you don't understand the reason of," and my husband was a very wise man.'

'Of course, of course, you are quite right, and can't understand why I offer five florins for looking at old ragged umbrellas.'

'Just so; for five florins you might see something better.'

'Well, it is very simple after all. My father had a very old umbrella to which he was much attached, and I heard that it had come by chance into your husband's hands, and I should very much like to have it as a souvenir.'

'And who was your father, sir? Perhaps I may have heard of him.'

The lawyer blushed a little.

'Pál Gregorics,' he said.

'Ah, Gregorics! Wait a bit! Yes, I remember, the funny little man in whose will . . .'

'Yes, yes. He left 2,000 florins to nine ladies in Besztercebánya.'

'I remember, but I don't think he had a son . . .'

'Yes . . . no . . . of course not . . . I mean . . .' and here he stopped in confusion. 'I am Gyuri Wibra, lawyer.'

Now it was Mrs Müncz's turn to be confused.

'Of course, sir, I understand. How stupid of me! I have heard of you, sir, and I knew your poor father, dear me, how very like him you are, and yet so handsome. I knew him very well,' she added smiling, 'though he did not leave me 2,000 florins. I was an old woman when he was still young. Well, sir, please go up and look at the umbrellas. I will show you the way, and tell you just where to look for them. Follow me, please, and I hope you will find the old gentleman's umbrella.'

'I would give you fifty florins for it, Mrs Müncz.'

At the words 'fifty florins' the old woman's eyes shone like two glow-worms.

'Oh! what a good son!' she sighed, turning her eyes up to heaven. 'There is nothing more pleasing to God than a good son who honours the memory of his father.'

She got quite active and lively at the thought of the fifty florins, and shutting the door of the shop, she tripped across the yard with Gyuri to the ladder of the loft, and even wanted to go up with him herself.

'No, no, stay down below, Mrs Müncz. What would the world say if we two were to go up to the loft together?' said Gyuri jokingly.

Old Rosalia chuckled.

'Oh, dear heart alive!' she said, 'there's no danger with me. Why, your father didn't even remember me in his will, though once upon a time . . . (and here she complacently smoothed her grey hair). Well, my dear, please go up.'

Gyuri Wibra searched about amongst the rubbish on the loft for quite half an hour, during which time the old woman came twice to the foot of the ladder to see if he were coming down. She was anxious about the fifty florins.

'Well?' she asked, as he appeared at last empty-handed.

'I have looked through everything,' he said, in a discouraged tone, 'but the umbrella I want is not amongst the others.'

The old Jewess looked disappointed. Her double chin began to tremble, her eyes were rapidly blinking.

'What can that silly Jónás of mine have done with it?' she lamented. 'Fifty florins! Dreadful! But then, he never had the instinct for doing the right things.'

'In all probability your husband used that umbrella himself. Mr Sztolarik of Besztercebánya says he distinctly remembers seeing him with it once.'

'What was it like?'

'The stuff was red, with patches of all sorts on it, and it had a pale green border. The stick was of black wood, with a bone handle.'

'May I never go to Heaven!' exclaimed Rosalia, 'if it was not the very umbrella he took with him last time he left home! Yes, I know he took that one!'

'It was a great pity he took just that one.'

Rosalia felt bound to defend her husband.

'How was he to know that?' she said. 'He never had the instinct for doing the right thing.'

'Well, there's no help for it now,' sighed Gyuri, as he stood on the last rung of the ladder, wondering what he was to do next, and feeling like Marius among the ruins of Carthage, only there were not even ruins to his Carthage; all hopes had returned to the clouds from which they had been taken.

Slowly he walked through the shop to his dogcart, which was waiting outside, and the old woman waddled after him, like a fat goose. But once in the street, she suddenly seemed to wake up, and seized hold of the lawyer's coat.

'Wait a bit, I had nearly forgotten it, but my son Móricz, who is a butcher in Ipolyság, is here at the moment; he has come to buy some sheep. My son Móricz knows everything, and may I never go to Heaven (Rosalia evidently had a strong objection to leaving this world), if he can't throw some light on the subject. Go to the fair, my dear boy, to the place where the sheep stand, and speak to the handsomest man you see there, that will be my son, Móricz; he's handsome, very handsome, this Móricz. Speak to him, and promise him the fifty florins. May I never go to Heaven if he didn't once tell me something about that umbrella. For when my poor dear Jónás got lost, Móricz went to look for him, and when he found traces of him, he went from village to village making inquiries, till everything was clear. (Here Rosalia gazed tearfully heavenwards.) Oh, Jónás, Jónás, why did you treat us so? If your senses had left you, why must you follow them? You had enough sons who would have taken care of you!'

This was Gyuri's last ray of hope, so he left the old woman without wasting another word and hurried along the rows of stalls to the scene of the fair which was right at the back of the church.

After putting a few questions to the bystanders, he found Móricz Müncz, a short, stout man, his pock-marked face looking like a turkey's egg. He was as ugly as a faun. His butcher's knife and steel hung from a belt round his waist, and on his arm was tattoed the head of an ox.

He was just bargaining for a cow, and its owner, a tanner, was swearing by heaven and earth that such a cow had never been seen in Bábaszék before.

'It will eat straw,' he assured him, 'and yet give fourteen pints of milk a day!'

'Rubbish!' answered Móricz. 'I'm not a calf, and don't intend to look upon this cow as my mother. I'm a butcher, and want to kill it and weigh it.'

'That's true,' said the honest tanner; and of his own free will he lowered the price by five florins.

Móricz did not seem to think that enough, and began poking at the ribs of the cow.

'What bones!' he exclaimed disappointedly, and then pulled open its mouth to look at its teeth. 'Why, it has not got a tooth in its head!'

'What do you want it to have teeth for?' asked the honest tanner. 'I don't suppose you want to weigh its teeth too?'

'But it kicks!'

'Well, it won't kick once it is killed, and I don't suppose you want to weigh it before it is killed?'

The honest tanner laughed at his own wit, which had put him into such a good humour that he again took five florins off the price. But Móricz was not yet satisfied, for he still gazed at the cow, as though trying to find more faults in her. And just at that moment Gyuri Wibra called out in Hungarian:

'Mr Müncz, I should like to have a word with you.'

The tanner, fearing to lose his purchaser, took five florins more off the price, and Móricz, being a sensible man, at once struck the bargain; in the evening, he always bought from people who had not been able to sell their cattle during the day, and gave it for a low price.

'What can I do for you, sir?'

'I should like to buy something of you, which belongs neither to you nor to me.'

'There are plenty of things in the world answering to that description,' said Móricz with a grin, 'and I can assure you, I will let you have it as cheap as possible.'

'Let us move on a bit.'

Gyuri led him out of the crowd to the village pump, near which grew an elder-tree. This tree, round which they had put some palings, was also a part of the future greatness of Bábaszék, for the green evil-smelling insects which housed in its branches, and which are used in various medicines (Spanish flies), induced people to believe that they might, once upon a time, have a chemist in Bábaszék. The young girls of the town used to collect the insects and sell them to the chemist at Zólyom for a few kreutzers; but that was forbidden now, for the people had decided, 'Near that tree there will once be a chemist's shop, so we will not have the insects taken away.'

They evidently considered them the foundation of the future chemist's store.

Gyuri told the Jew what he wanted; that he was interested in his father's favourite umbrella, and would buy it if he could find it. Did Móricz know anything about it?

'Yes, I do,' was the disappointed answer, for now he knew what a trifle it was, and he saw the price fall in proportion.

'I will give you fifty florins for any information that will lead to its discovery.'

Móricz quickly took off his cap which until now he had not considered it necessary to remove. Fifty florins for an old umbrella! Why, this young man must be the Prince of Coburg himself from St Anton! Now he noticed for the first time how very elegantly he was dressed.

'The umbrella can be found,' he said, and then added more thoughtfully, 'I think.'

'Tell me all you know.'

Móricz reflected for some time. He had to sort out the rather confused memories he had of his late father.

'Let me see, where shall I begin? It is now about fourteen years since my father disappeared, and I have forgotten most of the details, but this much I remember that I started to look for him with my young brother, and in Podhrágy I found the first trace of him, and following this up, I was told that when there, he was still quite in his right mind, had sold a few trifles to the villagers, slept at the inn, and had bought a very old seal from a certain Raksányi for two florins. He must have had all his senses about him then, for when we took him out of the Garam, he had the seal in his coat pocket, and we sold it for fifty florins to an antiquary, as it turned out to be the seal of Vid Mohorai, of the time of the Árpád dynasty.'

'Yes, but these particulars have nothing to do with the subject in question,' interrupted the young man impatiently.

'You will see, sir, that they are of interest.'

'Well, perhaps so; but I don't see what they have to do with the umbrella.'

'You will see in time, if you will listen to the rest of my tale. I heard in Podhrágy that he went from there to Abellova, so I went there too. From what I heard, I began to fear that my father had started to lose his senses here, for he had always inclined towards melancholy. Here they told us that he had bought a lot of "angel kreutzers"* from the villagers for four kreutzers each; but later on I found I was mistaken in my surmise.'

'How was that? Was he not yet mad?'

'No, for a few days later, two young Jews appeared in Abellova, each bringing a bag of "angel kreutzers", which the villagers bought from them for three kreutzers each, knowing they were really worth four.'

'So it is possible . . .'

'Not only possible, but certain, that the two young cheats had told the honest old man to buy up all the "angel kreutzers" he could for them, and he thus became their confederate without knowing it. So it is very probable he may have been mad then, or he would have seen through the whole affair. From Abellova he went through the Visoka Hora forest to Dolinka, but we could find out nothing odd about his doings, though he spent two days

---

* Small coins, on which the crown of Hungary is represented, held by two angels; they were issued in 1867, many people wore them as amulets and believed they bring luck. (Translator's note.)

there. But in the next village, Sztrecsnyó, the children ran after him, and made fun of him, like of the prophet Elijah, and he, unfastening his pack (not the prophet Elijah, but my poor father), began throwing the various articles he had for sale at them. In fifty years' time they will still remember that day in Sztrecsnyó, when soap, penknives, strings of beads and mouth-organs fell amongst them like manna from heaven. Since then it is a very common saying there, "It was only once that there came a mad Jew to Sztrecsnyó".'

'Bother Sztrecsnyó, let us return to our subject.'

'I have nearly done now. In Kobolnyik my poor old father was seen without his pack; in one hand he had his stick, in the other his umbrella, with which he drove off the dogs which were set upon him. So in Kobolnyik he still had his umbrella, you see.'

Tears were rolling down Móricz's pock-marked face, his heart was quite softened at the remembrance of all these incidents. His voice, too, grew dull and extremely gentle.

'After that we looked for a long time for traces of him, but only heard of him again in Lehota. One stormy summer night he knocked at the door of the watchman's house, the last in the village, but when they saw he was a Jew, they drove him away. They told me he had neither a hat nor an umbrella then, only the heavy, rough stick he used to beat us with when we were children.'

'Now I begin to understand the drift of your remarks. You want to show that the umbrella was lost between Kobolnyik and Lehota.'

'Yes.'

'But that proves nothing, for your father may have lost it in the wood, or amongst the rocks, and if anyone found it, they would probably make use of it to put it in the arms of a scarecrow.'

'No, that is not it, I know what happened. I heard it by chance, for I was not looking for the umbrella; what did I care for that! I wanted to find my father. Well, amongst the Kvet mountains I met a tinker walking beside his cart, a very chatty man he seemed to be. I asked him, as I did everyone we met, if he had not seen an old Jew about there lately. "Yes," he answered, "I saw him a few weeks ago in Glogova during a downpour of rain; he was spreading an umbrella over a child left outside a small house, and when he had done so he moved on".'

The lawyer sprang up hastily.

'Go on,' he cried.

'There is nothing more to tell, sir. But from the description the tinker gave me, I am sure it was my father, and, besides, Glogova lies just between Lehota and Kobolnyik.'

'Well, you have given me valuable information,' exclaimed the lawyer, and, taking a fifty-florin note out of his pocket-book, he added: 'Accept this as a slight return for your kindness. Good-bye.'

And off he went like a hound which has just found the scent; over some palings he vaulted in order to get to his cart as quickly as possible. In he raced, but as he passed the gingerbread stall, Móricz Müncz stood before him again.

'Excuse me for running after you,' he exclaimed breathlessly, 'but it suddenly occurred to me that I might give you a word of advice, which is this. There are a good many people from Glogova here at the fair, so you really might get the crier to go round and find out if they know anything of the umbrella. If you would promise a reward for any information, in an hour's time you will have plenty, I am sure. In a small village like Glogova, everyone knows everything.'

'It is quite unnecessary,' replied the lawyer, 'for I am going to Glogova myself. Thanks all the same.'

'Oh, sir, it is I who have to thank you; you have behaved in a princely fashion. Fifty florins for such a trifle! Why, I would have done it for one florin.'

The lawyer smiled.

'And I would willingly have given a thousand, Mr Müncz.'

And with that he walked away, past Schramek's house with its blue-painted gate next to which the spruce young women from Zelevnyik were selling their hazelnut strings and wreaths of onions for which they were mostly paid not in money but in kind. Móricz stood gazing after him till he was out of sight.

'A thousand florins!' he repeated, shaking his head. 'If I had only known it!'

And off he went, driving the cow he bought of the tanner before him.

- I V -

The Ear-Ring

From the inn opposite Schramek's house lively sound proceeded. I beg pardon, I ought to call it 'hotel', at least, that is the name the inhabitants of Bábaszék delighted in giving it, and the more aristocratic of them always patronized it in preference to the other inns. The gipsies from Pelsőc were there, and the sound of their lively music could be heard far and wide through the open window. Handsome Slovak women in their picturesque dresses, with their pretty white headgear, and younger girls with red ribbons plaited into their hair, all run in to join the dance, and if the room is too full, late-comers take up their position in the street and dance there.

But curiosity is even stronger than their love of dancing, and all at once the general hopping and skipping ceases, as János Fiala, the town servant and crier, appears on the scene, his drum hung round his neck and his pipe in his mouth. He stops in front of the 'hotel' and begins to beat his drum with might and main. What can have happened? Perhaps the mayor's geese have strayed? Ten or twelve bystanders begin to ply him with questions, but Fiala would not for the world take his beloved pipe out of his mouth, nor would he divulge state secrets before the right moment came. So he first of all beat his drum the required number of times, and then with stentorian voice, shouted the following:

'Be it known to all whom it may interest that a gold ear-ring, with a green stone in it, has been lost, somewhere between the brick-field and the church. Whoever will bring the same to the Town Hall will be handsomely rewarded.'

Gyuri paused a moment at the sound of the drum, listened to the crier's words, and then smiled at the look of excitement on the peasant girls' faces.

'I am sure, I wouldn't give it back if I found it,' said one.

'I'd have a hairpin made of it,' said another.

'Heaven grant me luck!' said a third, turning her eyes piously heavenwards.

'Don't look at the sky, silly,' said another; 'if you want to find it, look at the ground.'

But as chance would have it, someone found it who would rather not have done so, and that someone was Gyuri Wibra. He had only walked a few steps when a green eye no bigger than a pea seemed to smile up at him from the dust under his feet. He stooped and picked it up; it was the lost ear-ring with the emerald in it. How tiresome, when he was in such a hurry! Why could not one of those hundreds of loitering people have found it? But the green eye looked so reproachfully at him that he felt he could not give way to his first impulse and throw it back into the dust, to be trampled on by some heavy boot. Who wore such fine jewellery here? Well, whoever it belonged to, he must take it to the Town Hall; it was only a few steps from there, after all.

He turned in at the entrance to the Town Hall where some leather watering-cans hung majestically from the walls, and pushed back in one corner there dejectedly stood a decrepit pillory (*sic transit gloria mundi!*), went up the staircase, and entered a room where the senators were all assembled round a green baize-covered table, discussing a serious and difficult question.

A most unpleasant thing had happened. The gamekeeper in the Liskovina Woods (the property of the town) had arrived there breathlessly not long before with the news that a well-dressed man had been found hanging on a tree in the wood; what was to be done with the body?

This was what was troubling the worthy senators and causing them to frown and pucker their foreheads. Senator Konopka declared that the correct thing to do was to bring the body to the mortuary chapel, and at the same time give notice of the fact to the magistrate, Mr Mihály Géry, so that he could tell the district doctor to dissect the body.

Senator Galba shook his head. He was nothing if not a diplomat, as he showed in the present instance. He said he considered it would be best to say nothing about it, but to remove the body by night a little further on, to the Kvaka Woods, which belonged to the Travnik district, and let *them* find the body.

Mravucsán was undecided which of the two suggestions to accept. He hummed and hawed and scratched his head, and then complained it was hot enough to stifle one, that he had gout in his hand, and that one leg of the senator's table was shorter than the others. This latter was soon remedied by putting some old deeds under the short leg. While they did so, he waited to see which side would have the majority, and as it turned out it was on Galba's side. But the Galba party was again subdivided into two factions. The strict Galba faction wanted the dead man's body smuggled over to the Travnik district. The moderate Galba faction, headed by András Kozsehuba, would have been contented with merely taking down the body, and burying it under the tree; they wanted, at all costs, to prevent it being carried through the village to the cemetery, which would certainly be the case if the magistrate were informed of the circumstances. For if a suicide were carried through a place, that place was threatened with damage by hail!

'Superstitious rubbish!' burst out Konopka.

'Of course, of course, Mr Konopka, but who is to help it if the people are so superstitious?' asked Senator Fajka, of the Kozsehuba faction.

Konopka wildly banged the table with his fat, beringed hand, upon which everyone was quiet.

'It is sad enough to hear a senator say such a thing! I can assure you, gentlemen, that the Lord will not send His thunderclouds in our direction just on account of that poor dead body. He will not punish a thousand just men because one unfortunate man has given himself to the devil, especially as the dead man himself would be the only one not hurt by the punishment! That wouldn't be a godly act at all!'

Mravucsán breathed freely again at these wise words, which were evidently not lost on the magistrates; he hastened to make use of the opportunity, and as once the tiny wren, sitting on the eagle's wings, tried to soar higher than the eagle, so did Mravucsán try to rise above the senators.

'What is true, is true,' he said, hitching his belt in place, 'and I herewith rule on the strength of the arguments put forward that there will be no hail.'

Up sprang Mr Fajka at these words.

'That is all the same to us,' he said, 'if matters stand so, let us have hail by all means, for when once all the townsfolk are insured by the Trieste Insurance Company, I see no difference whether there is hail or not. In fact, it would be better if there were some, for, if I know our people well, they will immediately go and insure the harvest far beyond its worth if the dead body is taken through the village. So the hail would not be such a great misfortune, but the carriage of the corpse through the village would be.'

He was a grand debater after all, that Senator Fajka, for he had again hit the nail on the head, and at the same time enlightened the Galba and the Kozsehuba factions.

'What a brain!' they exclaimed.

The word brain reminded Galba of the dissecting part of the business—*per associationem idearum*—and he at once began to discuss the point.

'Why dissect the man? We know who he is, for it is as plain as piecrust that he is a greedy agent for some insurance company, and has hanged himself here in our neighbourhood in order to make people insure their harvest. It's as clear as day!'

'You are mad, Galba,' said Konopka crossly.

Upon which the senators all jumped up from their places, and then the noise broke forth, or, as Fiala, the town servant and crier, used to say, 'they began to boil the town saucepan', and every eye was fixed on the mayor, the spoon which was to skim the superfluous froth.

But the mayor drew his head down into the dark blue collar of his coat, and seemed quite to disappear in it; he gnawed his moustache and stood there helplessly, wondering what he was to say and do now, when all at once the door opened, and Gyuri Wibra stood before them. In spite of all folks may say, the powers above always send help at the right moment to save the face of the great.

At the sight of the stranger, who, an hour or two before, had wanted to buy an old umbrella of Mrs Müncz, the mayor suddenly pushed back his chair and hurried towards him (let the senators think he had some important business to transact with the newcomer).

'Ah, sir,' he said hurriedly, 'you were looking for me, I suppose?'

'If you are the mayor, yes.'

'Of course, of course!' (Who else could be mayor in Bábaszék but Mravucsán, he wondered?)

'They have been crying the loss of an ear-ring, and I have found it. Here it is.'

The mayor's face beamed with delight.

'Now that is real honesty, sir. That is what I like. This is the first ear-ring that has been lost since I have been in office, and even that is found. That's what I call order in the district.'

Then turning to the senators, he went on:

'It is only an hour since I sent the crier round the town, and here we have the ear-ring. They couldn't manage that in Budapest!'

Just then he noticed that the stranger was preparing to leave.

'Why, you surely don't mean to leave us already, sir? There is a reward offered for the finding of this ear-ring.'

'I do not want the reward, thank you.'

'Oh, come, don't talk like that, young man, don't run away from luck when it comes in your way. Is it not written in one of the Epistles: "Your gold and silver is cankered"? You know the story of the poor man who gave his luck away to the devil without knowing it, and how sorry he was for it afterwards?'

'Yes, he was sorry for it,' answered the lawyer, smiling, as he remembered the fable, 'but I don't think we can compare this case with that.'

'I am sure you have no idea to whom the ear-ring belongs.'

'Not the slightest. Whose is it?'

'It belongs to the sister of the Glogova priest.'

Gyuri screwed up his mouth doubtfully.

'Don't be too quick in your conclusions; just come here a minute; you won't repent it.'

'Where am I to go?'

'Come into the next room.'

The mayor wanted to keep him there at any cost, so as to gain time before deciding as to the dead man's future. He took the young man's arm and propelled him towards the door.

'But, my dear sir, I have important business to get through.'

'Never mind, you must come in for a minute,' and with that he opened the door and all but pushed the young man into the other room.

'My dear young lady,' he called out over Gyuri's shoulder, 'I have brought you your ear-ring!'

At these words a young girl turned from her occupation of putting cold water bandages on the shoulder of an elderly lady, lying on a sofa.

Gyuri was not prepared for this scene, and felt as confused and uncomfortable as though he had committed some indiscretion. The elder woman, partly undressed, was lying on a sofa, her wounded right shoulder (a remarkably bony and unalluring one) was bare. The young man at the door stammered some apology and turned to go, but Mravucsán held him back.

'Don't go,' he said, 'they won't bite you!'

The young girl, who had a very pretty, attractive face, hastened to throw a cloak over her companion, and sprang up from her kneeling position beside the lady. What a figure she had! It seemed to Gyuri as though a lily, in all its simple grandeur, had risen before him. 'This gentleman has found your ear-ring, and brought it you back, my dear.'

A smile broke over her face (it was as though a ray of sunlight had found its way into the mayor's dark office), she blushed a little, and then made a curtsey, a real schoolgirl curtsey, awkward and yet with something of grace in it.

'Thank you, sir, for your kindness. I am doubly glad to have got it back, for I had given up all idea of ever seeing it again.'

And taking the ear-ring in her hand she held it up between two fingers and began to swing it as if it were the visible tongue of a tiny invisible bell, and followed its movement by rocking the beautiful head. She was a child still, though full grown, you could see it in every movement. Gyuri felt he ought to say something, but found no suitable words.

This child disconcerted him, but there was something delightful in her artless manner which quite charmed him. And some peculiar sweet fragrance that pervaded the 'chancery' (as the simple ordinary room was called by the local people so fond of exaggeration) overpowered him. There he stood, helpless and speechless, as though he were waiting for something. Perhaps for hearing the sound of the invisible bell. Or was it the reward he wanted? The silence was getting painful, and the position awkward. At last the girl saw that the young man did not move, so she broke the silence.

'Oh dear! I had nearly forgotten in my delight that I had offered . . . I mean . . . How am I to say it?'

It now occurred to Gyuri (for danger electrifies the tired brain) that she was offering him the reward, so he thought it timely to cut her short by making known his name.

'I am Dr Wibra,' he said, 'from Besztercebánya.'

'Oh, how lucky!' exclaimed the girl, clapping her hands glee-fully. 'We are just in want of a doctor for poor madame.'

This little misunderstanding was just what was wanted. As blotting-paper will absorb ink, so did it swallow all embarrassment. Gyuri smiled.

'I am very sorry, my dear young lady; I am not a doctor of medicine, but merely a doctor of law.'

The young girl looked disappointed at this announcement, and blushed a little at her mistake; but Mravucsán was quite excited.

'What's that I hear? You are young Wibra, the noted lawyer? Well, that is nice! Who would have thought it? Now I under-stand. (He tapped his forehead.) Of course, you are here to try and find out particulars about one of your cases. I might have thought of it when I met you at Mrs Müncz's. Of course, a gentleman like you must have some special reason for buying an old umbrella. Well, the fates must have sent you here now, for we are discussing such a very difficult question in the next room that our minds are too small for it. How strange, Miss Veronica, that your ear-ring should be found by such a renowned lawyer.'

Veronica stole a look at the 'renowned lawyer', and noticed for the first time how handsome he was, and how gentlemanly, and her heart began to beat at the thought that she had nearly offered him the five florins Mravucsán had suggested for a reward.

Mravucsán hastened to offer the lawyer a chair, cast an anxious look round his office, and remarked with horror what an untidy state it was in; deeds lying about everywhere, coats and cloaks, belonging to the senators, empty glasses and bottles, for they were in the habit of drinking a glass now and then when they had settled some particularly important business, which was quite right of them, for the truth that emanated from them must be replaced by a fresh supply, and as the Hungarians say, 'There is truth in wine.'

The sight of that office would really have discouraged Mr Mravucsán if his eye had not at that moment fallen on the portrait of Baron Radvánszky, the lord lieutenant of the county, hanging on the wall in front of him. That, after all, lent some distinction to the room. He wished from his heart that the baron's image came to life to see what an illustrious guest they were harbouring.

But as the baron was not inclined to come to life, Mravucsán felt it devolved on him to express his satisfaction.

'I am a poor man,' he said, 'but I would not accept a hundred florins in place of the honour that is done to my poor office today. It is worth something to have the most renowned lawyer in the county, and the prettiest young lady . . .'

'Oh, Mr Mravucsán!' exclaimed Veronica, blushing furiously.

'Well,' said Mravucsán, 'what's true, is true. One need not be ashamed of being pretty. I was good-looking myself once, but I was never ashamed of it. Besides, a pretty face is of great use to a girl, isn't it, Mr Wibra?'

'Yes, it is a very lucky thing,' answered Gyuri quickly, coming out of his reverie.

Mravucsán shook his head.

'Let us simply say it is a great help, for luck can easily turn to misfortune, and misfortune to luck, as was the case now, for if it had not been for today's accident, I should not now have the pleasure of seeing you all here.'

'What is that?' asked Gyuri. 'An accident?'

Veronica was going to answer, but that talkative mayor put on his word again.

'Yes, there was an accident, but in a short time there will be no traces of it, for the ear-ring is here, madame's shoulder is here, it will be blue for some days, but what the devil does that matter, it is not the colour that makes the shoulder. And the carriage will be all right too, when the smith has mended it.'

'So the horses that were running away with a broken carriage . . .?'

'Were ours,' said Veronica. 'They took fright near the brick-field, the coachman lost his hold of the reins, and when he stooped to gather them up, he was thrown out of the carriage. In our fright we jumped out too, I did not hurt myself, but poor madame struck her shoulder on something. I hope it will be nothing serious. Does it hurt very much, Madame Kriszbay?'

Madame opened her small yellow eyes, which till then had been closed, and the first sight that met them was Veronica's untidy hair.

'Smooth your hair,' she said in French in a low voice, then groaned once or twice, and closed her eyes again.

Veronica, greatly alarmed, raised her hand to her head, and found that one of her plaits was partly undone.

'Oh, my hair!' she exclaimed. 'The hairpins must have fallen out when I jumped out of the carriage. What am I to do?'

'Let down the other plait,' advised Mravucsán. 'That's it, my dear; it is much prettier so, isn't it, Mr Wibra?'

'Much prettier,' answered Gyuri carelessly, casting a glance at the two black, velvety plaits, with a lovely dark bluish tinge on them, which hung nearly down to the edge of her flounced millefleurs skirt.

So that was the Glogova priest's sister. Incredible! Perhaps he was dreaming. This was by no means his idea of priests' sisters. He always pictured them as fat, waddling red-faced spinsters who as time went by came to resemble their brothers, smelled of pomade and developed double chins.

The lawyer thought it was time to start a conversation.

'I suppose you were very frightened.'

'Not very; in fact, I don't think I was frightened at all. But now I begin to fear my brother will be anxious about me.'

'The priest of Glogova?'

'Yes. He is very fond of me, and will be so anxious if we do not return. And yet I hardly know how we are to manage it.'

'Well,' said Mravucsán consolingly, 'we have the horses, and we will borrow a cart from someone.'

Veronica shuddered and shook her head, the dazzling black plaits tossing rhythmically around her shoulders.

'With those horses? Never again!'

'But, my dear young lady, you must never take horses seriously, they have no real character. You see, this is how it was. Near the brickfield there is that silly windmill, for, of course, every town must have one. The world is making progress, in spite of all Senator Fajka says. Well, as I said, there is the windmill. I had it built, for everyone made fun of us because we had no water in the neighbourhood. So I harness the wind to do the job. Of course, the horses don't understand that; they are good mountain horses, and had never seen a beast with such enormous wings, turning in the air. Small wonder they were frightened and ran away. You can't blame them for it. But they will have forgotten all about it by now and will take you quietly home.'

'No, no, I'm afraid of them. Oh, how dreadful they were! If you had only seen them! I won't go a step with them. As far as I am concerned, I could walk home, but poor Madame Krisz-bay . . .'

'Now that would be a nice sort of thing to do,' remarked Mravucsán. 'Fancy my allowing my best priest's little sister to walk all the way home with those tiny feet of hers! That would be a nice thing to do indeed! How she would stumble and trip over the sharp stones in the mountain paths! And his reverence would say: "My friend Mravucsán is a nice sort of fellow to let my sister walk home, after all the good dinners and suppers I have given him." Why, I would rather take you home on my own back, my dear, right into Glogova parish!'

Veronica looked gratefully at Mravucsán, and Gyuri wondered, if it came to the point, would Mravucsán be able to carry out his plan, or would he have to be carried himself. The mayor was an elderly man, and looked as though he were breaking up.

He found himself glancing curiously at the old gentleman, measuring his strength, the breadth of his chest, and of his shoulders, as though the most important fact now were, who was to take Veronica on his back. He decided that Mravucsán was too weak to do it, and smiled to himself when he discovered how glad this thought made him.

It is astonishing in how many idle directions the mind is apt to stray, and how meandering the channels of thought are from which the first drops of love break forth.

Mravucsán's voice broke in upon his musings.

'Well, my dear,' he was saying, 'don't you worry yourself about it; take a rest first, and then we will see what is to be done.

Of course, it would be better to have other horses, but where are we to get them from! No one in Bábaszék keeps horses, we only need oxen. I myself keep oxen. For a mountain is a mountain, and horses are of no use there, for they can, after all, only do what an ox can, namely, walk slowly. You can't make a grand show here with horses, and let them gallop and prance about, and toss their manes. This is a serious part of the country, yes, I repeat it, a serious part. The chief thing is to pull, and that is the work of an ox. A horse gets tired of it, and when it knows the circumstances it loses all pleasure in life, and seems to say, 'I am not such a fool as to grow for nothing. I'll be a foal all my life.' And the horses round about here are not much bigger than a cat, and are altogether wretched-looking.'

He would have gone on talking all night, and running the poor horses down to the ground, if Gyuri had not interrupted him.

'But I have my carriage here, Miss Veronica, and will take you home with pleasure.'

'Will you really?' exclaimed Mravucsán. 'I knew you were a gentleman. But why on earth didn't you say so before?'

'Because you gave me no chance to put in a word edgeways.'

'That is true,' laughed Mravucsán good-humouredly. 'So you will take them?'

'Of course, even if I were not going to Glogova myself.'

'Are you really going there?' asked Veronica, surprised.

'Yes.'

She looked at him thoughtfully for a minute, and then said, holding up a finger in childish threat:

'Don't try to deceive us.'

Gyuri smiled.

'On my word of honour, I intended going to Glogova. Shall we all go together?'

Veronica nodded her head, and was just going to clap her hands for joy like the child she was, when madame began to stir on the sofa, and gave a deep sigh.

'Oh dear,' said Veronica, 'I had quite forgotten madame. Perhaps, after all, I can't go with you.'

'Why not? The carriage is big enough, there's plenty of room.'

'Yes, but may I?'

'Go home? Who is to prevent it?'

'Why, don't you know?'

'Who?' asked Gyuri surprised.

'Etiquetted.'

(Gyuri burst into a laugh. Oh, what a little simpleton she was!)

'Yes, yes', she assured them, seeing they were laughing at her, for Mravucsán's face too twisted into a wide grin, 'it says in the book on etiquette: "You must not accept the arm of a stranger." '

'But a carriage is not an arm,' burst out Mravucsán. 'How could it be? If it were, I should have two carriages myself. My dear child, leave etiquette to look after itself. In Bábaszék I decide what is etiquette, not the French mamselles. And I say a carriage is not an arm, so there's the end of it.'

'Of course, you are right, but all the same, I must speak to madame about it.'

'Just as you like, my dear.'

Veronica again knelt down by the sofa, and a whispered conversation ensued, the result of which was, as Gyuri understood from the few French words he could hear, that madame quite shared Mravucsán's view of the case, that a carriage is not an arm, and that if two people have been introduced to each other, they are not strangers, and consequently, in Madame Kriszbay's opinion, they ought to accept the young man's offer. Besides, in times of danger there is no such thing as etiquette. Beautiful Blanche Montmorency on the occasion of a fire was saved by the Marquis Privadière with nothing on but her night-gown, and yet the tower of Notre Dame is still standing!

Gyuri felt as impatient as a card-player when the cards are being dealt, and a large stake has been placed on one of them, until at length Veronica turned round.

'We shall be very thankful if you will take us in your carriage,' she said smiling, as she was sure Blanche Montmorency would have done so under the same conditions. Gyuri received the announcement with eager expectation and was at once itching to go.

'I will go and see after the carriage,' he said, taking up his hat. But Mravucsán stood in his way.

'Oh, no, you don't,' he said. '*Pro primo*, even if Veronica can go, I am sure Madame Kriszbay cannot start yet; it would be a sin to make her drive now; she must rest a bit first, after her fright and her bruises. If my wife puts some of her wonderful plaster on it tonight, she'll wake twenty years younger in the morning. *Pro secundo*, you can't go because I won't allow you to. *Pro tertio*, because it is getting dark. Please look out of the window.'

He was right; the sun had disappeared behind the dark blue lines of the Zólyom Hills, and the fir-trees in front of the Town Hall cast their long shadows down the road, right up to the Mravucsán garden, where a lean cat was performing its evening ablutions amongst the oleanders.

All the same, the lawyer began to plead (it was part of his business).

'It will be a quiet, warm night,' he said. 'Why should we not start? After all, it can make no difference to madame whether she groans in bed or in the carriage.'

'But it will be dark,' objected Mravucsán, 'and there are some very bad bits of road between here and Glogova, and two or three precipices. In spite of my being mayor, I cannot order moonlight for you.'

'We don't need it; we can light the lamps.'

Veronica seemed undecided, and glanced from one to the other of the gentlemen after each weighty argument, till at length Mravucsán put in the finishing touch.

'There will be a storm tonight, for there is the dead body of a man hanging on a tree by the road. You will see it when you pass through the wood.'

Veronica shuddered.

'I would not go through that wood by night for the life of me,' she exclaimed.

That settled the question. Gyuri bowed, and received a bright smile in return, and Mravucsán rushed into the next room and told

Konopka to take his place (oh, his delight at getting rid of his responsibility!), as he had visitors, and had no time to think of other things; then he whispered in the ears of some of the senators (those who had on the best coats), that he would be pleased to see them for supper at his house and then rushed home to give orders for the reception of the distinguished guests. On the staircase he caught sight of Fiala and sent him to drive the lawyer's dogcart, which stood in front of Mrs Müncz's shop, to his courtyard.

After a few minutes, Mrs Mravucsán appeared at the Town Hall to take the ladies home with her. She was a short, stout, amiable woman whose broad, smiling face spoke of good temper and kind-heartedness. She was dressed like all women of the middle class in that part, in a dark red skirt and black silk apron, and on her head she wore a black silk frilled cap tied with a ribbon under her chin.

She entered the room noisily, as such simple village folks do.

'Well, I never!' she exclaimed. 'Mravucsán says you are going to be our guests. Is it true? What an honour for us! But I knew it, I felt it, for last night I dreamed a white lily was growing out of my basin, and this is the fulfilment of the dream. Well, my dear, get all your things together, and I'll carry them across, for I'm as strong as a bear. But I forgot to tell you the most important thing which I really ought to have said at the beginning: I am Mrs Mravucsán. Oh, my dear young lady, I should never have thought you were so pretty! Holy Virgin! Now I understand her sending down an umbrella to keep the rain off your pretty face! So the poor lady is ill, has hurt her shoulder? Well, I've got a capital plaster we'll put on it; come along. Don't give way, my dear, it has to be borne. Why, I had a similar accident once, with Mravucsán driving too. We fell into a ditch, and two of my ribs were broken, and I've had trouble with my liver ever since. Such things will happen now and then. Does it hurt you very much?'

'The lady does not speak Slovak,' said Veronica, 'nor Hungarian.'

'Good gracious!' exclaimed Mrs Mravucsán, clasping her hands. 'So old, and can't even speak Hungarian! How is that?'

And Veronica was obliged to explain that madame had come direct from Munich to be her companion, and had never yet been in Hungary; she was the widow of a French officer, she added, for Mrs Mravucsán insisted on having full particulars. They had received a letter from her the day before yesterday, saying she was coming, and Veronica had wanted to meet her at the station.

'So that is how it is. And this . . . (Mrs Mravucsán nearly said "scarecrow", but caught herself in time) . . . this lady can't even speak Slovak nor Hungarian! Poor unhappy creature! And what am I to do with her?—whom am I to put next her at table?— how am I to offer her anything? Well, it will be a nice muddle! Luckily the schoolmaster can speak German, and perhaps the young gentleman can, too?'

'Don't you worry about that, Mrs Mravucsán, I'll amuse her at supper, and look after her wants,' answered Gyuri.

With great difficulty they got ready to go, Madame Kriszbay moaning and groaning as they tried to dress her, after having sent Gyuri into the passage. Mrs Mravucsán collected all the shawls, rugs, and cloaks, and hung them over her arm.

'We will send the servant for the lady's box,' she said.

Then she made madame lean on her, and with some difficulty they managed to get her downstairs. Madame was complaining, half in French, half in German, and the mayor's wife chattered continually, sometimes to the young couple walking in front, sometimes to madame, who, with her untidy hair, looked something like a poor sick cockatoo.

'This way, this way, my dear young lady. That is our house over there. Only a few more steps, my dear madame. Oh, the dog won't bite you. Go away, Garam! We shall be there directly. You will see what a good bed I will give you to sleep in tonight; such pillows, the softest you can imagine!'

It made no difference to her that Madame Kriszbay did not understand a word of what she was saying. Many women talk for the sake of talking. Why should they not? They are probably afraid a spider might spin its web before their mouth if they keep silent.

'It hurts you, does it not? But it will hurt still more tomorrow; that is always the way with a bruise of that kind. Why, you will feel it in two weeks' time.'

Then, casting a sly glance at the pair walking in front:

'They make a handsome couple, don't they?'

It was not far to the Mravucsán house, and it would have been nearer still if there had not been an immense pool of water just in front of the Town Hall, to avoid which they had to go a good bit out of their way. But this pool was a necessity, for all the geese and ducks in the village swam on it, the pigs came and wallowed in the mud round it, and last but not least, the firemen took their water from here in case of fire. And I nearly forgot to say that all the frogs from the whole neighbourhood had taken up their abode in it, and gave splendid concerts to the townsfolk.

So, as I said before, they needed the pool and gladly put up with its presence, and it was considered common property. Once a civil engineer, János Nepomuk Brunkusz, had been travelling this way, and he had called their attention to the fact that the pool ought to be filled up; but they just laughed at him, and left it as it was.

So now they had to go right round the pool to the 'hotel', which strangers always named the 'Frozen Sheep', in reference to the climatic conditions at Bábaszék. The gipsies were still playing inside, and outside several couples were turning in time to the music, and some peasants from Túróc were standing about drinking their glass of brandy, while a waggoner from Zólyom sat alone at the only table drinking as hard as he could. He was already rather drunk, and was keeping up a lively conversation all by himself, gazing now and then with loving eyes at the lean horse harnessed to his cart, and which, with drooping head, was awaiting his master's pleasure to move on.

'My neighbour says,' philosophized the waggoner aloud, 'that my horse is not a horse. And why is it not a horse, pray? It was a horse in the time of Kossuth! What? It can't draw a load? Of course not, if the load is too heavy. It is thin, is it? Of course it is thin, for I don't give it any oats. Why don't I give it any? Why, because I have none, of course. What's that you say? The other day it couldn't drag my cart? No, because the wheel was stuck in the mud. My neighbour is a great donkey, isn't he?'

Upon which, up he got, and stumbled over to the Túróc peasants, requesting them to give their opinion as to whether his neighbour was a donkey or not. They got out of his way, so, like a mad dog, which sees and hears nothing but smells a human being, the waggoner rushed upon Madame Kriszbay.

'Is mine a horse, or is it not?'

Madame was frightened, and the smell of brandy, which emanated from the good man, made her feel faint.

'*Mon Dieu!*' she murmured, 'what a country I have come to!'

But Mrs Mravucsán, gentle as she was generally, could also be energetic if necessary.

'I don't know if yours is a horse or not,' she said, 'but I can tell you, you're a drunken beast!'

And with that she gave him a push which sent him rolling over on his back. He lay there murmuring:

'My neighbour says my horse is blind in one eye. Nonsense! He can see the road just as well with one eye as with two.'

Then up he got, and began to follow them with the unconscious stubbornness of the drunk, and Madame Kriszbay, leaving go of Mrs Mravucsán's arm, and in her fright forgetting her wounded shoulder, took to her heels and ran, with her skirt and petticoat raised awkwardly above her knees lest she should trip over them. The dancers seeing her went into fits of laughter at the pair of thin legs she showed.

'How on earth can she run so fast with such thin legs?' they asked each other.

Still more surprised were Veronica and Gyuri (who had seen nothing of the incident with the waggoner), they could not imagine why the sick woman was running at the top of her speed.

'Madame! Madame! What is the matter?'

She gave no answer, only rushed to the Mravucsán house, where she again had a fright at the sight of three enormous watchdogs, who received her with furious barks.

She would have fallen in a faint on the floor, but at that moment Mravucsán appeared on the scene to receive his guests, so she fell into his arms instead.

The good mayor just held her quietly, with astonished looks, for he had never yet seen a fainting woman, though he had heard they ought to be sprinkled with water, but how was he to go for water? Then he remembered he had heard that pinching was a good remedy, that it would, in fact, wake a dead woman; but in order to pinch a person, she must have some flesh, and Madame Kriszbay had nothing but bones. So he waited with Christian patience till the others arrived on the scene, and then gave her up to their tender mercies.

'Oh!' she whispered again and again, 'what a country I have come to!'

PART FOUR

Intellectual Society in Bábaszék

- I -

The Supper at the Mravucsáns'

I do not intend to expatiate on what followed. The miracle that the clothes grew with the child only happened to Christ. The same mantle he had worn as a little boy covered his body when he was treading towards the Golgotha with heavy steps.

No mantle like that has been seen ever since (and the tailors are grateful for it), but a similar wonder is time and again worked by long-winded novelists; from stuff that would at best do for a waistcoat, their pen is apt to patch up a complete wardrobe.

But I am not fond of drawing things out too great a length, so I will only give a short description of the Mravucsán supper, which was really excellent, and if anyone were discontented, it could only have been Madame Kriszbay, who burned her mouth severely when eating of the first dish, which was lamb with paprika.

'Oh,' she exclaimed, 'something is prickling my throat!'

But the pudding she found still less to her taste (a plain paste rolled out very thin, and cut into squares, boiled and served up with curds and whey, and small squares of fried bacon).

'*Mon Dieu!*' she said, 'it looks like small bits of wet linen!'

Poor Mrs Mravucsán was inconsolable at her guest's want of appetite.

'It is such a disgrace for me,' she complained.

Then it occurred to her to offer her some of her preserved fruit and to this madame seemed to take a fancy, for she finished up the dish, and in proportion as her hunger was appeased, her liking for her surroundings increased.

She had the Lutheran clergyman, Sámuel Rafanidesz, on her right, and the schoolmaster, Teofil Klempa, on her left, and to them was deputed the task of entertaining the unfortunate foreigner. Their invitations had been put in this form:

'You must come, for there is to be a German lady at supper, whom you are to entertain.'

And they did all they could to prove to the rest of the company how much at ease they were in good German society.

Madame Kriszbay seemed very contented with her neighbours, especially when she discovered that the Rev. Sámuel Rafanidesz was a bachelor. What! did clergymen marry there? (Perhaps, after all, she had not come to such a bad country!)

The schoolmaster was a much handsomer man, but he was older, and was, besides, married. He had an intelligent face terminating in a long, flowing black beard that covered his chest; he had, too, a certain amount of wit, which he dealt out in small portions.

Madame Kriszbay smiled at his sallies. Poor woman! She would have liked to have laughed at them, but did not dare to, for her throat was still burning from the effects of that horrid paprika, or perhaps only from the unpleasant memory of it. Now and then her face (which was otherwise like yellow wax) got quite red from the efforts she made to keep from coughing, which, besides being the forerunner of old age, she also considered very demeaning.

'Don't mind us, my dear,' called out the mayor's wife, 'cough away as much as you like. A cough and poverty cannot be hidden.'

Madame began to feel more and more at home, for as it turned out, the clergyman had been at school at Munich, and could tell a lot of anecdotes of his life there, in the Munich dialect, much to madame's delight.

The Rev. Sámuel Rafanidesz did not belong to the stiff, sanctimonious order of clergymen, and though there was a Slovak sentence composed by Teofil Klempa, often repeated by the good people of Bábaszék, which bore reference to him, and which, if read backwards, gave his name: 'Szedi na fare, Rafanidesz' ('Stay in your parish, Rafanidesz'), he never took this advice, and had already been sent away from one living (somewhere in Nógrád) because of an entanglement with some lady in the parish. Mrs Mravucsán knew the whole story, and even the lady, a certain Mrs Bahó.

She must have been a silly woman, for it was she herself who let the cat out of the bag, to her own husband, too; and she was not a beauty either, as we can see from Mrs Mravucsán's words:

'Rafanidesz was a fool to take up with her. You should never ask a kiss from an ugly woman, nor a loan from a poor man, for they immediately go and boast of it.'

Thus Mrs Mravucsán. It is true, she added:

'But if anyone were to call me as a witness, I should deny the whole thing.'

So you see, I can't stand good for the truth of it either. But that is neither here nor there.

Madame Kriszbay certainly enjoyed the company of her two neighbours, and those learned gentlemen soon raised the whole country in her estimation. But it was lucky she understood no Slovak, and could not hear the less lofty conversation carried on by the rest of the invited worthies of Bábaszék. Of course, they were clever people, too, in their way, and Veronica often smiled at the jokes made, for they were all new to her, though the natives of Bábaszék knew them all by heart; for instance, the rich butcher, Pál Kukucska, always got up when the third course was on the table, and drank to his own health, saying in a deep, guttural voice:

'Long life to my wife's husband!'

It would really be waste of time to try and describe the supper, for nothing of any real importance happened. They ate, they drank, and then they went home. Perhaps they spoke of important matters? Not they! Only a thousand trifles were discussed, which it would be a pity to put in print; and yet the incidents of that supper were the talk of Bábaszék for weeks after. For instance, Mr Mravucsán upset a glass of wine with the sleeve of his coat, and whilst they were wiping it up, and strewing salt on the stain, Senator Konopka, turning to the lady of the house, exclaimed:

'That means a christening, madam!'

Of course Mrs Mravucsán blushed, but Veronica asked in the most innocent tone:

'How can you know that?' (She was either a goose, that young girl, or she was a good actress.)

Now who was to answer her with a face as innocent as the Blessed Virgin's must have been when she was a girl in short frocks?

They all looked at each other, but luckily the forester's wife, Mrs Wladimir Szliminszky, came to the rescue with this explanation:

'You see, my dear, the stork which brings the children generally lets one know beforehand, and the knocking over a glass is one of the signs it gives.'

Veronica thought for a bit, then shook her beautiful head, which seemed to be surrounded by a halo of innocence, unbelievingly.

'But I saw the gentleman knock the glass over himself,' she objected.

To this Mrs Szliminszky had no answer ready, so according to her usual custom she turned to her husband and began worrying him.

'Wladin, cut the fat off that meat.'

Wladin frowned. The Adam's apple was running up and down his scrawny neck—a sign of silent disagreement.

'But, my dear, that is just the best bit.'

'Never mind, Wladin, I can't allow it. Your health is the first consideration.'

And Wladin obediently cut off the fat bits.

'Why is your coat unbuttoned? Don't you feel how cold it is? Button it up at once, Wladin.'

The forester did as he was told, and with the pleasant feeling of having done his duty, turned his attention to his plate again.

'Not another bit, Wladin, you've had enough. We don't want you to dream of bulls tonight.'

Wladin obediently put down his knife and fork, and prepared to drink a glass of water.

'Give it me first,' cried his wife excitedly. 'I want to see that it is not too cold.'

Wladin handed over his glass of water.

'You may drink a little of it, but not too much. The less muck in the stomach the better. Oh Wladin, you are drinking like a fish. Stop, stop, that will do!'

Poor Wladin! He was a martyr to conjugal love! For sixteen years he had suffered under this constant thoughtfulness, and though he was a strong man when he married, and had never been ill since, yet every minute of his life he expected some catastrophe; for, through constant warnings, the unfortunate Pole had worked himself up to the belief that a current of air, or a drop of water could be disastrous to him. He felt that malignant Nature was lying in wait for him in a thousand shapes.

'Take care, Wladin, or the dog will bite your foot!'

One of the watchdogs was under the table gnawing at a bone he had possessed himself of, and a little further off the cat was looking on longingly as much as to say, 'Give me some of that superfluous food!'

Now began the so-called *amabilis confusio*. Everyone spoke at once, and everyone about a different subject. The senators had returned to the important question of the corpse hanging in the wood; Mrs Mravucsán complained that no one was eating anything, and looked as wretched as she could.

Each one drank to the other's health, and during the quiet moment that followed, a voice was heard:

'Oh, Wladin, Wladin!'

It was Mrs Szliminszky's voice; she evidently objected to her husband drinking, and her neighbour, Mr Mokry, the lawyer's clerk, objected to her constant distractions, in spite of the interesting theme they were discussing.

'That strong cigar will harm you, Wladin, you had better put it down. Well, and why did you go to Besztercebánya, Mr Mokry?'

'I had a lot to do there, but, above all, I bought the suit I have on.'

He looked admiringly at his dark blue suit for about the hundredth time that evening.

'It is a very nice suit. What did you pay for it?'

'I had it made to measure at Kléner's and went to try it on myself.'

'What was the price?'

'It is real Gács cloth, and quite impervious to rain; you should see it by daylight!'

'Yes, of course, but what did it cost?' asked the Polish lady, her thoughts still occupied with her husband.

'I saw the piece of cloth myself; this was the first length cut off it. It has a peculiar look in the sunlight.'

'Yes, yes; but I asked the price of it.'

But it was difficult to bring Mokry to think of other things when he was once launched on the subject of his new suit.

'Kléner has a tailor working for him, a certain Kupek, who used to work at one of the court tailor's in Vienna, and he said to me: "Don't grudge the money, Mr Mokry, for this is such a durable stuff that your own skin will wear out first." Please feel it.'

'It's as soft as silk . . . Wladin, my dear, I think you had better change places with me. You are in a draught there each time the door is opened. What are you making such a face for? You surely don't mean to argue with me? Over you come now!'

The martyr to conjugal love changed places with his wife, and now Mrs Szliminszky was on the opposite side of the table, next to Wibra; but he was entirely taken up with Veronica, who was chattering to her heart's content. The clever young man, of whom it was said he would once be deputy for Besztercebánya, was listening to the girl with as much attention as though a bishop were speaking, and would not for a moment have taken his eyes off her.

They spoke quietly as though they were discussing very important questions, though they were actually speaking of the most innocent things. What did Veronica do at home? She read a good deal, and took long walks. What did she read, and where did she walk? And Veronica gave the titles of some books. Gyuri had read them all too, and they began exchanging notes regarding some of them, such as 'Elemér the Eagle', 'Iván Berend', 'Aranka Béldi'. Gyuri considered Pál Béldi very stupid for not accepting the title of prince when it was offered him. Veronica thought it was better he had not done so, for if he had, the novel would never have been written.

Then Gyuri began to question her about Glogova. Was it very dull? Veronica looked at him, surprised. How could Glogova be dull? It was as though some ignorant person had asked if Paris were dull.

'Is there a wood there?'

'A beautiful one.'

'Do you ever go there?'

'Of course.'

'Are you not afraid?'

'Afraid of what?'

'Well, you know, woods sometimes have inhabitants one might be afraid of.'

'Oh, but the inhabitants of our woods are more afraid of me than I of them.'

'Can anyone be afraid of you?'

'Oh, yes, they are, because I catch them.'

'The robbers?'

'Don't be so silly, or I shall be cross!'

'I should like to see what you look like when you are cross.'

'Well, I shall be if you talk such rubbish again. I catch butterflies in the wood.'

'Are there pretty butterflies there? I had a collection when I was a student; I believe I have it still.'

At this a desire for rivalry seized hold of Veronica.

'You should see my collection,' she said. 'I have all kinds. Tigers, Admirals, Apollos; only, it is such a pity, my Apollo has lost one of its wings.'

'Have you a Hebe?'

'Oh yes, it is nearly as big as the palm of my hand.'

'And how big is that? Let me see it.'

Veronica spread out her hand on the table; it was not so very big after all, but fine and pink as a rose-leaf. Gyuri took a match and began to measure it, and in doing so, accidentally touched her hand with his finger, upon which she hastily drew it away and blushed furiously.

'It is very hot,' she said, putting up her hand to her hot face, as though she had drawn it away for that purpose.

'Yes, the room has got quite hot,' Mrs Szliminszky broke in. 'Unbutton your coat, Wladin!'

Wladin heaved a sigh of despair, and undid his coat.

Veronica returned to the subject of the butterflies.

'I think butterfly-catching must be the same to me as hunting to a man.'

'I am very fond of butterflies,' answered Gyuri, 'because they only love once.'

'Oh, I have another reason for liking them.'

'Perhaps because of their moustaches?'

Veronica turned her head away impatiently.

'Mr Wibra, you are beginning to be unpleasant.'

'Thank you for the compliment.'

'What compliment?'

'You say I am beginning to be unpleasant, which is as much as to say I was pleasant till now.'

'Oh, the legal mind at work. I see it is dangerous to talk with you, for you put words into my mouth I never intended saying. I shall not speak again.'

'I'll never do it again, never, I assure you. Only do talk,' pleaded Gyuri.

'Do butterflies really interest you?'

'Upon my honour, they interest me more at this moment than lions and tigers.'

'I think butterflies are so pretty—like a beautifully dressed woman. And what tasteful combinations of colour. I always look at their wings as though they were so many patterns of materials. For instance, look at a Hebe, with its black and red under-wings, don't they match beautifully with the yellow-and-blue dress! Believe me, renowned Worth might with advantage take a walk in the woods, and learn the art of combining shades from the butterflies.'

'Gently, Wladin!' called out Mrs Szliminszky at this moment. 'How many lungs have you? A three-kreutzer stamp is sufficient for local letters.'

Wladin and Senator Fajka were wondering how matters would stand if they were both very deaf, and Wladin was talking so loudly that his loving spouse felt bound to put in a word of remonstrance, and request him to have some respect for his lungs.

'They are quite close to each other, and yet they shout, the same thing as though they were to put a fifteen-kreutzer stamp on a local letter. Oh dear! When will people be more sensible!'

At that moment Senator Konopka rose and drank to the health of the host, the 'regenerator' of Bábaszék. He spoke in exactly the same thin, piping voice as Mr Mravucsán; when the guests closed their eyes, they really believed the master of the house himself was speaking, and sounding his own praises; of course, this caused great amusement. Upon that, up sprang the mayor, and answered the toast in Konopka's voice, with just the same grimaces and movements he always made, and the merriment rose in proportion. Kings do this too in another form, for at meetings and banquets they pay each other the compliment of dressing up in each other's uniforms; and yet no one thinks of laughing at them.

Toast succeeded toast.

'You have let the dogs loose now,' whispered Fajka to Konopka.

Mokry drank to the health of the lady of the house and then Mravucsán stood up a second time to return thanks in his wife's name. He remarked that, to their great disappointment, one of those invited had been unable to come, namely Mrs Müncz, who had at the last moment had an attack of gout in her foot, which was no wonder, considering the amount of standing and running about she did when there was a fair in their town. Then they all emptied their glasses to the health of the old Jewess of Bábaszék.

After the shouts of acclamation had died away, Wladin Szliminszky called out:

'Now it is my turn!'

'Wladin, don't make a speech!' cried his wife. 'You know it is bad for your lungs to speak so loud.'

But she could do nothing now to prevent him; a henpecked husband is capable of everything; he will button or unbutton his coat, eat or drink to order, but refrain from making the speech his brain has conceived he will not; at least, it has never yet been heard of in the annals of Hungarian history.

'I take up my glass, gentlemen, to drink to the fairest flower of the company, beloved by God, who on one occasion sent down His servant from Heaven, saying: "Go down at once, Peter, with an umbrella; don't let the child get wet." Long life to Miss Veronica Bélyi.'

Veronica was as red as a rose, especially when the guests all got up one after the other, and went and kissed her hand; some of them even knelt to do it, and pious Mrs Mravucsán bent down and kissed the hem of her dress.

Gyuri thought at first on hearing Wladin's peculiar speech that the good man had gone mad, and now seeing everyone following his example, was more surprised than ever, and a strange uneasy feeling crept over him.

'What miracle is it your husband is referring to?' he asked, turning to Mrs Szliminszky.

That good lady looked at him surprised.

'What! Don't you know the story? Why, it is impossible. It is even printed in Slovak verse.'

'What is printed?'

'Why, the story of the umbrella . . . Wladin, you are very hot, your face is the colour of a boiled lobster. Shall I give you my fan?'

'What about the umbrella?' queried Gyuri impatiently.

'It is really strange you have never heard anything about it. Well, the story runs that when your fair neighbour was a little child, they once left her under the eaves of the priest's house. Her brother, the priest of Glogova, was in the church praying. A storm came on, it poured in torrents, and the child would have been wet through and have got inflammation of the lungs, or something of the kind, if a miracle had not taken place. An old man appeared on the scene, no one knows from where; he seemed to have fallen from Heaven, and he spread an umbrella over the child's head.'

'My umbrella!' burst unconsciously from the lawyer.

'What did you say?'

'Nothing, nothing.'

His blood coursed more quickly through his veins, his heart beat faster, he raised his head quickly, with the result that he also knocked his glass over.

'A christening, another christening!' called out everyone.

'My best wishes,' said Mr Rafanidesz, turning to Mrs Szliminszky, who blushed becomingly and told him not to talk nonsense.

'It is not true, is it, Wladin?' she turned to her husband for support.

But the young lawyer would not let such nonsense divert the conversation from his favourite topic; he drew his chair nearer to hers, and said, his voice trembling with suspense:

'Please go on.'

'Well, the grey-haired man disappeared, no one knew how nor where, and those who saw him for a moment swore it was St Peter.'

'It was Müncz!'

'Did you speak?'

Gyuri bit his lip, and saw that he had spoken his thoughts aloud.

'Nothing, nothing; please go on.'

'Well, St Peter disappeared, and left the umbrella behind him.'

'And does it still exist?'

'I should think it does indeed. They keep it as a relic in the church of Glogova.'

'Thank God!'

Gyuri drew a deep breath as though a great weight had fallen from him, and wiped heavy beads of perspiration off his forehead.

'Found!' he murmured absently. He thought he would have fallen from his chair in his joy. Everything was clear now, but unexpected luck crushed him. He felt his neck stiffen, his heart jump, his ears tingle.

'And to whom does it belong? To the Church?' he asked.

'It may be yours once,' said Mrs Szliminszky teasingly. 'It will be Veronica's when she marries; the priest of Glogova told me so himself. "It will belong to my sister," he said, "unless she makes a present of it to the Church when she marries." '

'Oh, no,' said the lawyer, shaking his head. 'At least, I mean . . . What am I saying? What were we speaking about? It is fearfully warm, I'm stifling. Please Mr Mravucsán, could we have the window open?'

'Of course,' and the mayor ran to open it.

'Button up your coat, Wladin!'

A fresh spring air entered by the window, and a naughty breeze put out both the candles.

'Kisses allowed,' called out Klempa in the sudden darkness.

A branch of lilac was just outside the window, and spread its delicious perfume through the room, decidedly more pleasant than the fumes of tobacco smoke which had filled it a minute before.

Madame Kriszbay, startled by the sudden darkness gave vent to a little scream, and Klempa seized the opportunity to exclaim:

'I assure you it was not I!'

There was a general confusion in the darkness, but Mrs Szliminszky, wanting to prove she was above being troubled by such trifles, quietly continued her conversation with Gyuri. This, of course, went to prove that she was using her mouth for speaking and, consequently, not for some other occupation.

'It is a pretty little legend, Mr Wibra. I am not easily imposed upon, and besides, we are Lutherans (though we keep that to ourselves); but I must say it is a very pretty legend. And the umbrella is really wonderful. Sick people are cured if they stand under it; a dead man rose to life again when it touched him. It is of no use your shaking your head, for it is true. I know the man himself, he is still alive. Altogether the things that umbrella has done are wonderful, especially the fact that it has brought luck and riches to the priest of Glogova.'

A dark suspicion took possession of Gyuri, and when the candles were re-lighted, it was to be seen he was as pale as death.

'Is the priest rich?' he asked.

'Very rich,' answered Mrs Szliminszky.

He drew nearer to her, and suddenly seized hold of her hand, pressing it convulsively. The good lady could not make out why. (If he had done so a minute sooner, she could have understood it, but the candles were alight now!)

'He found something in the umbrella, did he not?' he asked, panting.

Mrs Szliminszky shrugged her white shoulders, half visible through the lace insertion of her dress.

'Why, what could he find in an umbrella? It is not a box, nor an iron case. But for the last fourteen years people have come from great distances to be married under the umbrella, and they pay generously for it. And then when a rich person is dying anywhere along the Biela Voda, from the Szitnya right as far as Kriván, they send for the priest of Glogova to hear their confession, and after their death, to bury them under the umbrella.'

Veronica, to whom the mayor's wife had been showing her embroidered table-cloths, calling her attention to the fineness of the linen, now caught a few words of the conversation.

'Are you speaking of our umbrella?' she asked amiably, leaning towards them.

Gyuri and Mrs Szliminszky started.

'Yes, my dear,' answered the latter, slightly confused.

Gyuri smiled mischievously.

'I see,' said Veronica, 'you don't believe the story.'

'No, I do not.'

'Really?' asked the girl reproachfully; 'and why?'

'Because I never believe nonsense, and because . . .'

- 161 -

He had nearly said too much, but he kept back the words that rose to his lips, when he saw how wounded the girl appeared at his incredulity. She smiled, turned her head away, and gazed silently at her plate. Gyuri was silent too, though he felt inclined to cry out:

'I am rich at last, for in the handle of that umbrella there are unknown treasures.'

It is remarkable that if good luck befalls a man, his first wish (for he still has wishes, even if they are all fulfilled) is to communicate it to others; he would like trumpets sounded, heralds to be sent round to announce it to the whole world. But then comes doubt, the everlasting 'perhaps'. And so it was with Gyuri.

'What is the umbrella like, Miss Veronica?' he asked.

Veronica closed her lips firmly, as though she considered it unnecessary to answer him, then thought better of it, and said:

'It is not much to look at; it is of faded red stuff, looks a thousand years old, and is patched all over.'

'With a border of small green flowers?'

'Have you seen it?'

'No, I only asked.'

'Yes, there is a border of green flowers on it.'

'Could I see it?'

'Certainly. Do you wish to?'

'That is what I am going to Glogova for.'

'Why, if you don't believe in it?'

'Just for that very reason. If I believed in it I should not go.'

'You are a heathen.'

She drew her chair away from him, at which he at once became serious.

'Have I hurt you?' he asked contritely.

'No, but you frighten me,' and her lovely oval face expressed disappointment.

'I will believe anything you like, only don't be afraid of me.'

Veronica smiled slightly.

'It would be a shame not to believe it,' struck in Mrs Szliminszky, 'for it is a fact—there is plenty to prove it. If you don't believe that, you don't believe anything. Either the miracles in the Bible are true, and if so, this is true, too, or . . .'

But she could not finish her sentence, for at that moment Madame Kriszbay rose from the table, saying she was tired, and would like to retire to her room, and Mrs Mravucsán led her and Veronica to two small rooms opening on to the courtyard. In the doorway Gyuri bowed to Veronica, who returned it with a slight nod.

'Shall we start early in the morning?' he asked.

She bowed with mock humility, inclining her head to one side.

'As you like, you doubting Thomas,' she said.

Gyuri understood the reference, and answered in the same strain:

'It depends upon how long the saints sleep.'

Veronica turned her head, made a face, and shook her fist playfully at him.

'I will pay you out!' she said.

Gyuri could hardly take his eyes off her, she looked so pretty as she spoke. Let the saints look like that if they could!

Soon after the Szliminszky pair started for home, accompanied by a man carrying a lantern for there was no moon. Mrs Szliminszky had made Wladin put on a light spring coat, hung a long cloak over his shoulders, tied a big woollen scarf round his neck, and having ordered him only to breathe through his nose, once they were out, she turned to Gyuri again.

'Yes, it is a beautiful legend, it made a great impression on me.'

'Poor legends!' returned Gyuri. 'If we were to pick some of them to pieces, and blow the gilt off them, the saintly odour, the cloud of mystery, what strange and simple truths would be left at the bottom.'

'Well, they must not be picked to pieces, that is all. Wladin, turn up the collar of your coat.'

The lawyer thought for a minute.

'Perhaps you are right,' he murmured with a faraway look on his face.

After a short time Gyuri also asked to be shown to his room.

'The magnet has gone!' muttered the lawyer's clerk.

Hardly had the door closed, when Kukucska, the butcher, exclaimed:

'Now we are free!'

He took off his coat, rolled up his sleeves, thus showing the head of an ox tattooed on his left arm, then winked knowingly at Mravucsán. The mayor seemed to understand the look.

'Right you are,' he commented beaming, 'before going to bed one ought to make sure if women still love him.'

With this he went to a cupboard and pulled out one of the drawers, from which he took a pack of cards.

The knave of spades was missing, but that did not make any difference to the intelligent members of Bábaszék society, for they had once before played 'Préférence' with those cards, and the last player had simply received one card less when they were dealt out, though he was supposed to have the knave of spades, and it was called the 'spirit card'. If they were playing spades, the last player in imagination threw the knave on it, saying: 'I play the spirit card!' But now, in view of the missing card, they decided to play a game of chance which lasted till daylight. The senators, the butcher, and the clergyman played, the lawyer's clerk served the drinks, and Klempa looked on, having no money to lose (schoolmasters being as a rule the poorest members of the community), and went from one player to the other, looking over their shoulders, and giving them advice what to play. But one after the other sent him away, declaring he brought them bad luck, which rather depressed him. So the poor schoolmaster wandered from one to the other, till at last he took a seat between the clergyman and the butcher, dropped his weary head on the table, and went to sleep, his long thick beard doubled up, and serving as a pillow. But he was to have a sad awakening, for that mischievous Pál Kukucska, seeing the beard on the table, conceived the idea of sealing it there; and fetching a candle and sealing wax, they dropped some on the beard in three places, and Mravucsán pressed his own signet ring on it. Then they went on playing, until he should awake.

Other incidents, and not very important ones either, were taking place in the house. Madame Kriszbay, to whom the mayor's wife had given her own bedroom, would not go to bed with the enormous eider-down quilt over her, for she was afraid of being suffocated during the night. She asked for a quilt, but Mrs Mravucsán did not possess such a thing, so inventive as she was she brought in her husband's enormous fur-lined cloak and threw it over madame, which so frightened the poor nervous woman that she was attacked by migraine, and the mayor's wife had to spend the night by her bed, putting horse-radish on her temples.

An unpleasant thing happened to Veronica, too. As soon as she was alone in the Mravucsáns' best bedroom, she locked the door, hung a cloak on the door-handle so that no one could look through the keyhole, drew the curtains across the tiny windows which opened on the courtyard, and then began to undress. She had unhooked the front of her bodice, releasing the whalebones—all acts which gave back the breasts and waist their true and even more enchanting contours. The last hook clicked open, the one that held the skirt fast above the hips, and the frilled garment began to slide downwards—like the envious green envelope peels off to reveal a rosebud.

Down swished the little skirt, which she was about to unfasten, when all at once she became aware of two bright eyes watching her intently and admiringly as though it had been a prince changed by some old witch into the form of a cat. Veronica, alarmed, clutched her open bodice with one hand, and hitched up the skirt (of which she was about to step out) with the other scolding the inquisitive visitor now in a plaintive, now in a peremptory tone of voice.

'Go along, you tiresome kitten,' she said, 'don't look at me when I'm undressing!'

She was such an innocent child, she was ashamed to undress before the kitten. She dressed again, and tried to drive it out of the room, but it hid itself under the bed, then jumped on a cupboard, and it was quite impossible to get rid of it. Mrs Mravucsán, hearing the noise from the next room, called out:

'What is the matter, my dear?'

'I can't drive the cat out.'

'Never mind her, she won't hurt you.'

'But she always watches me,' answered Veronica.

She put her candle out, and began to undress in the dark, but that tiresome cat walked into the middle of the room again, and her eyes shone more than ever.

'Wait a bit, you curious little thing,' said Veronica. 'I'll get the best of you yet.'

She made a barricade of chairs, then got inside it, as though she were in a fortress, and began to undo her boots. Do you think that barricade made any impression on the kitten? Not a bit of it. There it was again, on the top of the chairs, from there one jump took it on to the washing stand, and another on to Veronica's bed.

This was bad tactics, for Veronica caught it there by the scruff of its neck and while looking for something to bind round its head, she kept admonishing the kitten:

'I'll teach you watching girls while they are undressing. Don't you know, you little darling, that such a thing simply isn't done?'

At last she found a thick woollen shawl which she wrapped round the kitten's head.

'Now, kitty, stare at me if you can!'

And after that she managed to undress in peace.

- II -

Night brings Counsel

Whilst the two ladies were occupied with these trifles, and Klempa with his beard sealed to the table slept the sleep of the just, Gyuri had also undressed, and retired to his bed, but found it impossible to sleep. His undressing (don't be afraid) is not going to be described here in detail, for such a thing would be unpardonable as matters stand. Why, indeed? Don't ask me. It is ugly and, therefore, indescribable. The undressing of a woman—there is poetry in it. If it is well written, the reader has the illusion of inhaling the intoxicating fragrance of a woman's body from the pages and not the smell of printer's ink; but the undressing of a man, phew! The very idea of it! You are at liberty to compose an ode or a dithyramb for that matter to a skirt, but the word 'trousers' is unutterable. Why is it so? God only knows. And what does it prove? Perhaps that man is a less aesthetic creature than woman. Or, perhaps, it only goes to show that the person who first laid down the rules of decency and indecency was a big fool.

But it was worse than all that, that our hero could not sleep.

It was not from indigestion, for Mrs Mravucsán's excellent supper had not disagreed with him; it was his brain which was hard at work, going over all the incidents that had taken place that day. He seemed to have lived through years in the last few hours. What an age it seemed since he had looked for the umbrella in Mrs Müncz's shop! And it was found quite unexpectedly. God had given it into the charge of an angel.

From the umbrella his thoughts flew to the 'angel'.

She was a nice little thing, he decided; not a bit unpleasant like other girls of that age he knew who were stiff, constrained, affected creatures lacking youthful vitality. Veronica was an exception. And she seemed to have taken to him too.

He passed again in revision all her words, her movements, which were likely to support this belief, enjoying them again and again (for remembering had a sweetening effect), but as he followed the coloured thread of his thoughts backwards, sorting out smiles, friendly words, softened voice, encouraging glances, unwatched movements (what a heart-warming collection it was), he found certain signs of coldness and indifference here and there, so that with an effort he leapt over the border of dream-land into golden reality—back to the umbrella.

Indeed, he could call himself so happy now that he did not need to worry about the sentiments of a silly girl. He was a rich man now, a nabob beginning from today. He would live like a prince henceforward, spend the winter in Budapest, or on the Riviera, in Monaco, and the summer at Ostende; in fact, he would be a grand gentleman, and not even look at poor priests' sisters. (How tiresome it was, his thoughts would always return to Veronica.)

Sleep would not come, how could it be expected? One scheme after the other passed before his mind's eye, like the butterflies in the Glogova woods. And he chased them all in turn. Oh! if it were only daylight, and he could move on.

His watch was ticking on the table beside his bed; he looked at it, the hands pointed to midnight. Impossible! It must be later than that; his watch must be slow! Somewhere in the distance a cock crew, as much as to say, 'Your watch is quite right, Mr Wibra.' He heard faint sounds of music proceeding from the 'Frozen Sheep' in the distance, and someone on his way home was singing desperately the famous Slovak shepherd's song, which says:

No shepherd buys his mutton by the pound,
The sheep is not his who drives it around.

Gyuri lighted a cigar; the curling smoke and the words of the silly song gave a fresh turn to his thoughts. Indeed, often the sheep is not his. Well, how strangely the umbrella had been found —or rather it had not been found yet, it was not yet in his possession, and when he came to look at the facts, he decided he was not much nearer to it than he had been. Until now he had supposed it had been thrown away as a useless rag, and he had had little hope of finding it. And now, what had happened? Things were quite different to what they had imagined them; for as it turned out, the umbrella was a treasure, a relic in a church. What was to be done about it? What was he to say to the priest tomorrow? 'I have come for my umbrella?' The priest would only laugh at him, for either he was bigoted and superstitious, in which case he would believe St Peter had brought the umbrella to his sister, or he was a Pharisee, and in that case he would not be such a fool as to betray himself.

The wind was rising, and the badly fitting windows and door of the little room that had been allotted to him were rattling, and the furniture cracked now and then. He could even hear the wind whistling through the Liskovina Woods, not far from the house. The hanged man Mravucsán had spoken of was working there properly. Gyuri blew out the candle whose flame was reluctantly dancing to the wind's tune and lay down again under the big eider-down quilt, and imagined he saw the corpse, hanging from a tree, waving from side to side in the wind, and nodding its head at him, saying, 'Oh, yes, Mr Wibra, you'll be well laughed at in the parish of Glogova.'

The lawyer tossed about on the snow-white pillows from which an odour of spring emanated. (They had been out in the garden to air the day before.)

'Never mind,' he thought, 'the umbrella is mine after all. I can prove it in a court of justice if necessary. I have witnesses. There are Mr Sztolarik, Mrs Müncz and her sons, the whole town of Besztercebánya.'

Then he laughed bitterly.

'And yet, what am I thinking of? I can't prove it, for after all the umbrella does not belong to me, but to the Müncz family, for the old man bought it. So only that which is in the handle belongs to me. But can I go to the priest and say: "Your reverence, in the handle of the umbrella is a cheque for 200,000 or 300,000 florins, please give it to me, for it belongs of right to me." '

Then Gyuri began to wonder what the priest would answer. He either believed the legend of the umbrella and would then say: 'Go along, do! St Peter is not such a fool as to bring you a cheque on a bank from Heaven!' Or, if he did look in the handle and find the receipt, he would say: 'Well, if he did bring it, he evidently meant it for me.' And he would take it out and keep it. Why should he give it to Gyuri? How was he to prove it belonged to him?

'Supposing,' thought our hero, 'I were to tell him the whole story, about my mother, about my father, and all the circumstances attending his death. Let us imagine he would believe it from alpha to omega; of what use would it be? Does it prove that the treasure is mine? Certainly not. And even if it did, would he give it me? A priest is only a man after all. Could I have a lawsuit, if he would not give it me? What nonsense! Of course not. He might take the receipt out of the handle, and what proofs can I bring then that it was ever in it?'

The perspiration stood on his forehead; he bit the bed-clothes in his helpless rage. To be so near to his inheritance, and yet not be able to seize hold of it!

'Black night, give counsel!' was Gyuri's prayer. And it is best after all to turn to the night for help. Gyuri was right to ask its advice, for it is a good friend to thought. Among the Golden Rules should be written, 'Think over all your actions by night, even if you have decided by day what course to take!' For a man has night thoughts and day thoughts, though I do not know which are the better. I rather think neither kind is perfect. For daylight, like a weaver, works its colours into one's thoughts, and night covers them with its black wings. Both of them paint, increase and decrease things—in one word, falsify them. Night shows the beloved one more beautiful than she is, it strengthens one's enemies, increases one's troubles, diminishes one's joy. It is not kind of it; but night is sovereign, and is answerable to no one for its actions. Take things as they come, but do not put it aside when you are seeking the truth. Though, of course, you do not really seek the truth; even if it comes to meet you, you get out of its way. I ought to have said, do not despise the night when you are trying to find the way out of a thing. Night will show you what to do, without your even noticing it. If it can do it in no other way, it brings you gentle sleep, and gives you advice in dreams.

After a time the wind dropped, the music at the 'Frozen Sheep' ceased, and Gyuri heard nothing but a rhythmic murmur, and all at once he seemed to be in the woods of Glogova, chasing butterflies with Veronica.

As they ran on amongst the bushes, an old man suddenly appeared before them, with a golden crook, a glory round his head, and his hat hanging by a bit of string from his neck.

'Are you Mr Wibra?' he inquired.

'Yes; and you?'

'I am St Peter.'

'What do you want?'

'I wish to sign a receipt for your happiness.'

'For my happiness?'

'I see you cannot get your umbrella, and my friend Gregorics has asked me to help you. So I am quite willing to sign a paper declaring that I did not give the umbrella to the young lady.'

'It is very good of you, but I have neither paper nor ink here. Let us go back to the village.'

'I have no time for that; you know I have to be at the gates of Heaven, and I can't stay away for long.'

'Well, what am I to do, how am I to get my umbrella?'

St Peter turned his back, and began to walk back the way he had come, but stood still beside a large oak-tree, and made a sign to Gyuri to approach. Gyuri obeyed.

'I'll tell you what, my friend, don't think too long about it, but marry Veronica, and then you will have the umbrella too.'

'Come,' said Gyuri, catching hold of the golden crook. 'Come and ask her brother to give his permission.'

He pulled hard at the crook, but at that moment a strong hand seemed to pull him back and he awoke.

Someone was knocking at the door.

'Come in,' he said sleepily.

It was the Mravucsáns's farm servant.

'I've come for your boots,' he announced.

Gyuri rubbed his eyes. It was day at last, the sun was smiling at him through the window. His thoughts were occupied with his dream, every incident of which was fresh in his mind. He thought he could hear the dried leaves rustling, and St Peter's voice again saying:

'Marry Veronica, my friend, and then you will have the umbrella too.'

'What a strange dream,' thought Gyuri; 'and how very much logic it contains. Why, I might have thought of that solution myself!'

By the time Gyuri was dressed, it was getting late, and every member of the Mravucsán household was on foot. One was carrying a pail to the stables, another a sieve, and near the gate, which last night's wind had partly lifted off its hinges, Gyuri's coachman was examining the damage done. Seeing his master advancing towards him, he took off his hat with its ostrich feathers.

'Shall I harness the horses, sir?'

'I don't know yet. Here, my good girl, are the ladies up?'

'They are breakfasting in the garden,' answered the slender maid he had accosted. 'Please walk this way.'

'Well, then, you may harness, János.'

Gyuri found the ladies seated round a stone table under a large walnut-tree. They had finished breakfast, only madame was still nibbling a bit of toast. He was received with ironical smiles, and Veronica called out:

'Here comes the early riser!'

'That title belongs to me,' said Mravucsán, 'for I have not been to bed at all. We played cards till daybreak. Klempa is still asleep with his beard sealed to the table.'

'A nice sort of thing for grown-up folks to do!' remarked Mrs Mravucsán.

Gyuri shook hands with them all, and Veronica got up and made a deep curtsey.

'Good morning, early riser,' she said. 'Why are you staring at me so?'

'I don't know how it is,' stammered Gyuri, gazing at the girl's beautiful face, 'but you seem to me to have grown!'

'In one night?'

'You were quite a little girl yesterday.'

'You appear to be dazed!'

'I certainly am when I look at you.'

'You seem to be sleepy still. Is this the time of day to get up?'

The playful, gentle tone was delightful to Gyuri, and he began to be quite talkative, defending himself in a jocular way.

'I fell asleep for a short time, and if the servant had not woke me, I should be asleep still. Oh, if she had only waited five minutes longer!'

'Had you such a pleasant dream?' asked Mrs Mravucsán. 'Will you take some coffee?'

'If you please.'

'Won't you tell us your dream?'

'I was going to marry, in fact, had got as far as the proposal.'

'Did she refuse you?' asked Veronica, raising her head, the beauty of which was enhanced by the rich coronet of hair in which she had stuck a lovely pink.

'I don't know what would have happened, for at the critical moment the servant woke me.'

'What a pity, we shall never know how it would have turned out!'

'You shall know some time.'

'How?'

'I will tell you.'

'How can you do that? Dreams cannot be continued from one night to another like novels in a periodical.'

Gyuri drank his coffee, lit a cigar, and from out the cloud of smoke he replied in a mysterious voice, his eyes turned heavenwards:

'There are such dreams, as you will see. And how did you sleep?'

Mrs Mravucsán seized eagerly upon the question and began to tell in great detail the story of Veronica's adventure with the kitten.

Gyuri saw the charming scene in his mind's eye, and his heart jumped. Mr Mravucsán laughed, and poor Veronica was covered with blushes.

Mrs Mravucsán, finding the opportunity a good one, launched upon a little lecture.

'My dear child, exaggeration is never good, not even in modesty. You will have to get used to such things. What will you do when you are married? You will not be able to shut your husband out of your bedroom, and prevent him from undoing your bodice. You must get used to that too.'

'Oh dear!' exclaimed Veronica. 'How can you say such dreadful things!'

And, stopping her ears, she jumped up and ran away to the gooseberry-bushes, where her dress got torn. Thereupon there was a rush for needle and thread, and the confusion was heightened when the carriage drove up, the two handsome black horses pawing the ground impatiently.

No bad business to be a lawyer as it seems. (So young and already the owner of such horses, and all he did to get them was a lot of lying!)

Every living member of the household had some task allotted to her. Anka must wrap up the ham in a cloth, Zsuzsa must run and fetch the fresh bread that had been baked for the occasion. Someone else must bring knives and forks. Would they like a little fruit packed in the basket? The foreign lady would be glad of something of the kind. And should she put a small pot of jam in too?

'But my dear Mrs Mravucsán, we shall be at home by dinner-time.'

'And supposing something happens to prevent it? You never can tell!'

And off she went to her store-room, whilst the mayor tried to persuade them to stay for lunch or, at least, an hour longer; but it was of no use, the travellers had made up their minds to start; not even the possibility of seeing Klempa wake up would induce them to change their plans.

They got into the carriage, the two ladies on the back seat, and Gyuri on the box with the coachman. But Gyuri sat facing the ladies, his knees brushing Veronica's. Whether he would hold out in that 'uncomfortable' position till Glogova, remained to be seen.

'To Glogova,' said Gyuri to the coachman, and János cracked his whip and the horses started, but hardly were they out of the yard, when the mayor's wife came tripping after them, calling out to them at the top of her voice to stop. They did so, wondering what had happened. But nothing serious was the matter, only Mrs Mravucsán had unearthed a few apples in her store-room, with which she filled their pockets, impressing upon them that the beautiful rosy-cheeked one was for Veronica. Then they started again, with a great amount of waving of handkerchiefs and hats, until the house, with all its people, its smoking chimneys and its large walnut-tree, was out of sight.

As they passed Mrs Müncz's shop she was standing at the door in her white cap, nodding to them with her venerable grey head, which seemed cut into two parts by the broad-rimmed spectacles. At the smithy they were hammering away at the priest's broken chaise, and poured water over the hot irons which were hissing like snakes. Further on various objects, which had been left unsold at yesterday's fair, were being packed in boxes and then put in carts to be taken home again. They passed in turn all the tiny houses, with their brightly painted doors, on which the names of the owners were printed in circles. At the last house, opposite the future Jewish burial-ground, two pistol-shots were fired.

The travellers turned their heads that way, and saw Mr Mokry in his new suit, made by the noted tailor of Besztercebánya, with his hat in one hand, and in the other the pistol he had fired as a farewell greeting. On the other side of the road was the dangerous windmill, its enormous sails throwing shadows over the flowering clover-fields. Luckily it was not moving now, and looked like an enormous fly pinned on the blue sky.

There was not a breath of wind, and the ears of wheat stood straight and stiff, like an army of soldiers. Deep silence reigned over the fields. Only the sound of the horses' hoofs was to be heard, and the woods of Liskovina stretched before them like a never-ending green wall.

PART FIVE

The Third Devil

- I -

Maria Czobor's Rose, the Precipice, and the Old Pear-Tree

Madame Kriszbay was very much interested in the neighbourhood they were driving through, and asked many questions. They passed a small chapel in the wood, and Veronica explained that a rich innkeeper had once been killed there by robbers, and the bereaved widow had built this chapel on the spot.

'Perhaps out of gratitude?' suggested Gyuri.

'Don't be so horrid,' exclaimed Veronica.

The Liskovina Woods, with their slopes, valleys and glades, are quite like a park, with the exception that there is not much variety in the way of trees, the birch, the favourite tree of the Slovaks, being predominant. It is just as melancholically blond among the trees as are the flaxen-haired Ancsurkas and Bohuskas among the girls. But of flowers there were any amount. The ferns grew to a great height, the anthoxantum had flowered, and in its withered state filled the whole wood with its perfume. Amongst plants, as amongst people, there are some which are only pleasant and agree-able to others after their death. What a difference there is in various kinds of plants. There is the gladiola, the most important part of which is the bulb it hides under the earth; whoever eats it dreams of the future.

Much simpler is the ox-eyed daisy, for it will tell you without any ceremonies if the person you are thinking of loves you very much, a little, or not at all; you have only to pull off its snow-white petals one by one, and the last one tells you the truth.

These are not the odious breed of gardens, foreign offspring imposed upon Mother Earth (some of which she is reluctant to receive and must be kept in pots), but her own beloved children whom she has conceived in the winter months and brought to life in spring to the pleasure of all living creatures.

The wild pink is the magic table for the fickle tribe of wasps, the lily serves as a drinking cup for the birds, the large dandelion is the seesaw of the butterflies. For the Liskovina Woods are generous; they provide beds for insects in the bells of bluebells, offer strawberries to children looking for birds' nests; serving all according to their deserts, they produce nosegays for young girls, herbs for old women, berries for song-birds and the poisonous aconite for the wicked wolf, which the peasants in that part called the 'wolf-killer'.

Whether it ever caused the death of a wolf is doubtful, for wolves have their fair share of sense, and probably knowing something of botany, they tell their cubs: 'Don't touch the Aconitum Lycotinum, children; it is better to eat meat.'

It was delightful driving in the shady woods, though Madame Kriszbay was alarmed each time a squirrel ran up a tree, and was in constant fear of the robbers who had killed the rich innkeeper.

'Why, that was eighty years ago, madame! They are all dead.'

'Well, and their sons?'

She was restless till they had got clear of the wood and had come to the large barren plain of Oporc, with here and there a small patch of oats, stunted in their growth.

But after that her fears returned as they came to another wood, the far-famed 'Zelena Hruska', in the shape of a pear. Supposing robbers were to turn up there among those oaks?

And Gyuri was just wishing for their appearance while madame was thinking with horror of them. As he sat face to face with the girl, he decided to marry her—because of the umbrella. The girl was certainly pretty, but even had she not been so, the umbrella was worth the sacrifice. St Peter had told him what to do, and he would follow his advice. Superstition, at which he had laughed the day before, had taken possession of him, and made a place for itself amongst his more rational thoughts. He felt some invisible power pushing him on to take this step. What power was it? Probably St Peter, who had advised him in his dream to take it. But how was he to set to work? That was what was troubling him the whole time.

How convenient it would be if there were some romance nowadays, as in olden times or in novels; for instance, if robbers were now to appear on the scene, and he could shoot them down one after the other with his revolver, and so free Veronica, who would then turn to him and say:

'I am yours till death!'

But as matters were at present, he did not dare to take any steps in the right direction; the words he had so well prepared seemed to stick in his throat. Doubts arose in his mind; supposing she had not taken a fancy to him! Supposing she were already in love! She must have seen other men besides himself, and if so, they must have fallen in love with her. Something ought to happen to help matters on a little.

But no robbers came, there probably were none; it was a poor neighbourhood, nothing grew there, not even a robber.

After they had passed the wood, they saw an old castle amongst the trees, on the top of a hill. It was the castle of Szlatina, had formerly belonged to the Czobors, and was now the property of the Princes of Coburg.

They had to stop at an inn to feed the horses, and Veronica proposed their going to look at the castle, of which an old man had charge; he would show them over it. The innkeeper assured them some of the rooms were just as the Czobors had left them; in the court were a few old cannons, and in the house a collection of curious old armour, and some very interesting family portraits, amongst them that of a little girl, Katalin Czobor, who had disappeared from her home at the age of seven. Veronica was very interested in the child.

'And what happened to her?' she asked.

'The poor child has never turned up to this day!' sighed the innkeeper.

'And when was it she disappeared?'

'About three hundred years ago,' he answered with a smile, and then accompanied his guests up the steep mountain path that, flanked by lilac-bushes, led to the castle.

They were silent on their return, oppressed by the gloom of decay, only Madame Kriszbay remarking:

'What a mouldy smell there was in there.'

Veronica had caught sight of a beautiful rose on a large bush near the half-ruined walls of the bastion.

'What an exquisite flower!' she exclaimed.

The old caretaker had a legend about that too. From this spot beautiful Maria Czobor had sprung from the walls, and thrown herself down the precipice, for her father wished her to marry an officer in the Emperor's army, and she was in love with a shepherd. The latter had planted a rose-bush on this spot, and every year it bore one single blossom. Gyuri dropped behind the others, and begged the old man to give him the rose.

'My dear sir, what are you thinking of? Why, the poor girl's spirit would haunt me if I were to do such a thing!'

Gyuri took out his purse and pressed two silver florins into the man's hand, upon which, without further ado, he took out his knife, and cut the rose.

'Won't the young lady's spirit haunt you now?' asked Gyuri, smiling.

'No, because with part of the money I will have a mass said for the repose of her soul.'

Guyri ran after the ladies with the rose in his hand, and offered it triumphantly to Veronica.

'Here is Maria Czobor's rose,' he said. 'Will you give me your pink in exchange?'

But she put her hands behind her back, and said coldly:

'How could you have the heart to pick it?'

'I did it for your sake. Will you not exchange?'

'No; I would not for the world wear that flower; I should think I had stolen it from that poor girl.'

'Will you really not accept it?'

'No!'

Disheartened, Gyuri threw the rose away, and it rolled down the hillside in the dust and dirt.

Veronica gazed pityingly after the flower as long as it was visible, then turned angrily to Gyuri.

'Is that the way to treat a flower? Had it hurt you in any way?'

'Yes,' answered the lawyer shortly.

'Did it prick you?'

'It pricked me dead. It informed me of a very unpleasant fact.'

'What was it?'

'It whispered the continuation of my last night's dream to me.'

'What a little chatterbox!'

She turned her big eyes upon Gyuri and spoke in a jesting tone.

'I should have had a refusal!'

Veronica threw back her head and turned her eyes towards heaven.

'Poor Mr Wibra!' she exclaimed, her face drawn in mock compassion. 'What misfortune to be refused in a dream!'

'Pray go on, make as much fun of it as you like,' he said bitterly.

'And are you sure you would have been refused?'

'Yes, now I am sure of it,' he answered sadly. 'You might guess now of whom I dreamed.'

'Of me?' she asked surprised, and the smile died away on her lips. 'Of me?' she stammered again, then was silent, descending the hill quietly in madame's wake with bent head. She had lifted the skirt of her dress a little to prevent its dragging in the dust, and her little feet were partly visible as she tripped along with regular steps, treading on the grass and flowers, which, however, were not crushed by her footsteps, but rose again, perhaps even fresher and prouder than before, as she passed on.

A tiny lizard crossed their path, its beautiful silvery armour shining in the sunlight. But what a sad fate befell the little knight in armour; just at that moment a wrathful giant (the well-known lawyer of Besztercebánya) came that way, murmuring: 'Why should it live?' and bringing down a heavy heel severed the poor lizard's head from its body.

Veronica just then turned round, and saw the cruel action; she felt inclined to cry over the poor lizard, but did not dare to say anything, for she herself began to be afraid of this Goliath, so she only murmured under her breath: 'Wretch!'

When they were further down the hill she saw before her the rose he had thrown away; there it lay, dirty and dusty, among the stones by the roadside, and, obeying a sudden impulse, she bent and picked it up, blowing the dust off its rosy petals, and then she placed it in the bosom of her dress, where it seemed as though it were in its right place at last. She did not say a word, nor did she look at that dreadful Goliath, but turned away her head, so that he could not see her face. But Goliath was quite satisfied at seeing the rose where he had wished it to be, and out of gratitude would have liked to restore the lizard to life, but that was, of course, impossible.

At the foot of the hill the carriage was waiting and the travellers took their places again, this time with an uncomfortable feeling. Silently they sat opposite each other, one looking to the right, the other to the left, and if their eyes happened to meet they hastily turned them away. When they spoke, their remarks were addressed to Madame Kriszbay, who began to notice that something had happened.

But what? Only a few childish words to which their minds had given a more serious meaning than they were meant to have, and had increased in size just like Professor Hatvani's narrow cell in Debrecen, which the devil enlarged to such an extent that the whole town had place in it. Well, in those few words everything was contained.

But now something else happened. I don't know how it was, but I think a pin dropped, and at the same moment Veronica bent down as though to look for it. In doing so the pink fell out of her hair into Gyuri's lap, and he picked it up in order to return it to her. But she made him a sign to keep it.

'If it would not stay in my hair, and fell into your lap, you may as well keep it.'

Would it not have stayed in her hair? Was it quite an accident? thought Gyuri, as he smelt the flower. What a pleasant odour it had! Was it from her hair? And what odour the hair itself might have without the pink!

Now they were driving beside the Brána, the famed Brána, which quite shuts this part of the country off from the rest of the world, like an immense gate. That is why it is called the Brána, or gate. It is no common mountain, but an aristocrat among its kind, and in fine weather it wears a hat, for its summit is hidden in clouds. It is also given to perspiration; several small streams make their way down its side, flowing together at the foot, and making one broad stream.

'That is the Biela Voda,' explained Veronica to Madame Krisz-bay, 'we are not far from home now.'

They still had to drive through one wood, and then the little white cottages of Glogova would be before them deep down in the valley. But this was the worst bit of the road, crooked and curved, full of ruts and rocks, and so narrow that there was hardly room for the carriage to pass.

János turned round and said with a shake of his head:

'The brake is king in these parts!'

The brake. But there was no brake for the dogcart, therefore they were in danger. All that he told his master in this round-about way.

'Take care, János, that you don't upset us!'

Again and again János got down from his seat, to fasten one of the wheels firmly or release it, according to need, and now the horses had to move at a funeral pace, and sometimes the road was so narrow between two hills that they could see nothing but the blue sky above them.

'This place is only fit for birds,' muttered János.

'Don't you like this part of the country?'

'It is like a pock-marked face,' he replied. 'It is not the sort of place one would come to choose a wife.'

Gyuri started. Had the man discovered his intentions?

'Why do you think so?'

'My last master, the baron (János had been at some baron's before in Sáros County), used to say to his sons, and he was a clever man, too, "Never look for a wife in a place where there are good air and mineral springs but no gnats!" '

At this both Veronica and Gyuri were obliged to laugh.

'That's a real Sáros way of looking at things. But you see, you have vexed this young lady.'

'According to your theory I shall have to be an old maid!' said Veronica.

But János vigorously denied the possibility of such a thing.

'Why, dear me, that is not likely; why . . . you . . .'

He wanted to say something complimentary, but could not find suitable words, and as chance would have it, his next words were nearer to swearing than to a compliment, for the shaft of the carriage broke.

The ladies were alarmed, and Gyuri jumped down from his seat to see the extent of the damage done. It was bad enough, for it had broken off just near the base.

'What are we to do now?' exclaimed János. 'I said this place was only fit for birds, who neither walk nor drive.'

'Oh, that is nothing serious,' said Gyuri, who at that moment was not to be put out by a shaft, nor by a hundred shafts.

'Give me your axe, and you go and hold the horses. I'll soon bring you something to fasten the shaft to, and strengthen it.'

He took a short-helved axe out of the tool-box under the coachman's seat, said a few words to reassure the ladies, and then jumped the ditch by the side of the road, and waded his way through the thicket to the trees.

For there were some trees there, but they were as rare as the hairs on the head of an old man. First came a stunted birch, then a couple of hazelnut-bushes, then some blackthorn, then a bare piece of ground without any trees, and then again a few old, scattered trees as if left behind by a forest that had moved to other parts. The reddish-brown clay underfoot had long since spent its productive force; it yielded nothing but mushrooms and feather-grass. A parched patch on the mantle of Mother Earth was the Glogova hill.

So it was rather difficult to find a suitable tree; one was too big, another too small; so Gyuri went on and on in search of one, going round a breach here, a gully there, and got so far that soon the carriage was out of sight, and only Veronica's red sunshade was to be seen in the distance, like a large mushroom. At length his eyes fell on a young birch which grew near to a small precipice. It was too big for a seedling and too small for a tree, but well-grown and promising. All the same it must be sacrificed, and down came the axe.

But hardly had two or three blows been struck when a voice was heard, crying out:

'Reta! Reta!' (Help! Help!)

Gyuri started and turned round. Who had called? The voice seemed quite close, but no one was visible far and near.

Again the call for help was repeated, and now it seemed to come out of the earth, and Gyuri immediately concluded it came from the precipice, and ran towards it.

'Here I am!' he called out. 'Where are you and what is the matter?'

'I am down the precipice,' was the answer; 'help me, for God's sake!'

Gyuri looked down, and saw a figure there in a black coat, but he could not see much of it, for it would have been dangerous to have gone too near to the edge.

'How did you manage to get down there?'

'I fell in yesterday evening,' groaned the man in the black coat.

'What! Yesterday evening! And can't you get out?'

'It is impossible, for there is nothing to hold on to, and if I catch hold of any projecting bits, they give way, and I fall back with them.'

'You are in a bad way altogether! And has no one passed here since then?'

'No one comes this way. I was prepared for the worst when I heard the sound of blows in the neighbourhood. Thank God you came! Help me if you can, good man, whoever you may be, and I will reward you!'

'I will help you of course, with the greatest pleasure, but I must think first how to manage it. If I let down the trunk of a small tree could you climb up it?'

'I am very weak from want of sleep and from hunger,' answered the man, his voice getting weaker from shouting.

'Poor fellow! Wait a moment!'

He had suddenly remembered the apples Mrs Mravucsán had put in his pockets that morning.

'Hallo, there! Look out, I am going to throw down a few apples to go on with, whilst I think over what I am to do.'

He took the apples out of his pocket, and rolled them down one after the other.

All of a sudden he remembered that Veronica's was amongst them. Supposing she were vexed at his giving it away!

'Have you got them?'

'Yes, thank you.'

'Please don't eat the red one, it is not mine.'

'Very well, I will not eat it.'

'You seem to be of the better class?'

'I am the parish priest of Glogova.'

Gyuri, surprised, fell a step backwards. How strange! The parish priest of Glogova! Could anything more unexpected have happened?

'I will get you out, your reverence; only wait a few minutes.'

Back he ran to the carriage, which was waiting in the valley below. From this point the country round about looked like the inside of a poppy-head cut in two. He did not go quite up to the carriage, but as soon as he was within speaking distance, shouted at the top of his voice to János:

'Take the harness off the horses, and bring it here to me; but first tie the horses to a tree.'

János obeyed, grumbling and shaking his head. He could not make out what his master needed the harness for. He had once heard a wonderful tale of olden times, in which a certain Fatépő Gábor (Tree-felling Gábor) had harnessed two bears to a cart in a forest. Could Gyuri be going to do the same?

But whatever it was wanted for, he did as his master told him, and followed him to the precipice. Here they fastened the various straps together, and let them down.

'Catch hold of them, your reverence,' called out Gyuri, 'and we will pull you up.'

The priest did as Gyuri said, but even then it was hard work to get him up, for the ground kept giving way under his feet; however, at length they managed it.

But what a state he was in, covered with dirt and dust; on his face traces of the awful night he had passed, sleepless and despairing, suffering the pangs of hunger. He hardly looked like a human being, and we (that is, my readers and I) who knew him years before, would have looked in vain for the handsome youthful face we remember. He was an elderly man now, with streaks of grey in his chestnut hair. Only the pleasant, amiable expression in his thin face was the same. He was surprised to see such a well-dressed young man before him—a rarity on the borders of the Glogova woods.

'How can I show you my gratitude?' he exclaimed, with a certain pathos which reminded one strongly of the pulpit.

He took a few steps in the direction of the stream, intending to wash his hands and face, but he stumbled and felt a sharp pain in his back.

'I must have hurt myself last night, when I fell, I cannot walk very well.'

'Lean on me, your reverence,' said Gyuri. 'Luckily my carriage is not far off. János, you go on cutting down that tree, whilst we walk slowly on.'

They certainly did go slowly, for the priest could hardly lift his left foot, and frequently stumbled over the roots of trees which interwove the ground in a pattern resembling the Sultan's signature; apparently below the ground the forest was still there. But up there the huge trees of old had been supplanted by dwarfs; the spindle-tree reigned and the cranberry-tree, two miserable shrubs, a pair of highwaymen. The former at least boasted some eye-pleasing clusters of little reddish-white flowers, but the latter was only there to be a nuisance for the passer-by.

The carriage was some way off, so they had plenty of time for conversation and every now and then they sat down to rest on the trunk of a fallen tree.

'Tell me, your reverence, how did you come to be in this part of the country late at night?'

And then the priest related how he had expected his sister home yesterday, who had gone to meet her governess at the railway station. As time went on, and there were no signs of them, he began to feel anxious, and towards evening became so restless that he did as he had often done before, and walked to the borders of the little wood. He walked on and on, finding the way by keeping his eye on the hills on both sides, and listened for the sounds of wheels in the distance. All at once it occurred to him that they might have gone round by the Pribalszky mill, which was a longer but prettier way to Glogova, and Veronica, his sister, was fond of the shade there. Of course, that was what they had done, and they must have arrived at home long ago whilst he was looking for them. So the best way was to turn back at once, and in order to get home as soon as possible, he unfortunately struck across a side-path. In his haste he must have stepped too near to the edge of the precipice and had fallen in.

'My poor little sister!' he sighed. 'How anxious she must be about me.'

Gyuri would have liked to turn the priest's sorrow into joy.

'We will soon reassure the young lady, and your reverence will feel all right after a night's rest. In two or three days it will seem like an amusing incident.'

'But which might have ended in a horrible death if Divine Providence had not sent you to help me.'

'It really does seem as though Divine Providence had something to do with it. The shaft of my carriage broke, or I should never have come near that precipice.'

'If I live to be a hundred I shall never forget your kindness to me, and your name will always have a place in my prayers. But how thoughtless of me! I have not even asked you your name yet.'

'György Wibra.'

'The well-known lawyer of Besztercebánya? And so young! I am glad to make the acquaintance of such an honourable man, sir, who is revered in the whole of Besztercebánya; but I should be much more pleased if a poor man now stood before me, to whom I could give a suitable reward. But how am I to prove my gratitude to you? There is nothing I possess which you would accept.'

A cunning smile played around Gyuri's mouth.

'I am not so sure of that. You know we lawyers are very grasping.'

'Is there really something, or are you joking?' asked the priest diffidently.

The lawyer did not answer immediately, but walked on a few steps towards an old wild pear-tree, which had been struck by lightning, and not far from which the carriage was standing.

'Well, yes,' he answered then, slowly, almost in a trembling voice, 'there is something I would gladly accept from you.'

'And what is it?'

'It has just struck me that there is something in my carriage which you might give me.'

'In your carriage?'

'Yes, something you do not know of yet, and which I should be very happy to possess.'

The priest took him by the hand.

'Whatever it may be, it is yours!'

In another minute they had reached the pear-tree.

'There is my carriage.'

The priest looked that way, and saw first a red sunshade, then a black straw hat under it, with some white daisies in it, and beneath it a sweet, girlish face. It all seemed so familiar to him, the sunshade, the hat, and the face. He rubbed his eyes as though awaking from a dream, and then exclaimed, catching hold of the lawyer's arm:

'Why, that is my Veronica!'

The lawyer smiled quietly and bowed.

'That is,' went on the priest in his kind, gentle voice, 'for the future she is your Veronica, if you wish.'

By this time Veronica had seen and recognized her brother, had jumped out of the carriage and run to meet him, calling out:

'Here we are, safe and sound. How anxious you must have been! And our carriage is broken to bits; and oh! if you had only seen the horses! All sorts of things have happened, and I have brought Madame Kriszbay.'

The priest embraced her, and was glad she seemed to know nothing of his accident. How sensible of Gyuri not to have mentioned it.

'Yes, yes, my darling, you shall tell me everything in order later on.'

But Veronica wanted to tell everything at once, the carriage accident in Bábaszék, the supper at Mravucsáns' (oh yes; she had nearly forgotten, Mr Mravucsán had sent his kind regards), then today's journey, the loss of her emerald ear-ring and its recovery . . .

The priest, who was slowly beginning to understand things, here broke in upon her recital in a teasing tone.

'And did you give the finder of it a reward?'

She was silent at first at the unexpected question, then answered hurriedly:

'No, of course not, how can you think of such a thing? What was I to give? Besides, he would not accept anything.'

'I am surprised at that, for he has since then applied to me for a reward.'

'Impossible!' said Veronica, casting a side-glance at Gyuri. Strange doubts had arisen in her mind, and her heart began to beat.

'And what does he ask for?' she asked in a low voice.

'He wants a good deal. He asks for the ear-ring he found, and with it its owner. And I have promised him both!'

Veronica bent her head; her face was suffused with burning blushes, her nostrils quivered, her bosom heaved. With an effort she kept back her tears.

'Well? Do you give me no answer? Did I do right to promise, Veronica? Answer me!'

Gyuri took a step towards her, and said, in a low, pleading voice:

'Only one word, Miss Veronica!' then stood back self-consciously under the pear-tree one of whose storm-rent branches hung down limply and partly hid his face.

'Oh! I am so ashamed!' said Veronica in a hardly audible whisper.

She did not say another word, not a single one, but all of a sudden burst into tears. A breeze came up just then across the Brána, and shook the old pear-tree, which obediently shed its white petals, probably the last the old tree would bear, over Veronica's head and dress.

- II -

Three Sparks

You, Madame, sit in the carriage, and can understand nothing
of what is going on. The young lady entrusted to your charge
springs out of the carriage, runs up to a strange man in a long
black coat, throws her arms round his neck, and then they all
begin to talk with excited gestures, standing under the pear-tree.
Then your pupil comes back to the carriage, capering as a lamb,
her face flushed as a rose, arm in arm with the young man who
had found her ear-ring yesterday. All of this is so unexpected, so
surprising. And whilst they are mending the broken shaft, and
re-harnessing the horses, the man in the black coat, who turns out
to be the girl's brother, turns to you and whispers in your ear:

'Your pupil has just engaged herself!'

Good gracious! When and where? Why, now, under the tree!
Ah, Madame Kriszbay, you feel you ought to faint now, partly
because you are a correct woman, and consequently horrified at
the way the event had taken place, and partly because you have
fallen amongst such strange uneducated people; but your bottle

of Eau de Cologne is quite at the bottom of your travelling-bag, and so it will be better not to faint, now, but declare that it is very shocking all the same!

For though a tree is suitable for flirting under, or for declaration of love, it is not the right place to ask a parent or guardian for a girl's hand. The proper place for that (especially in novels) is a well-furnished drawing-room. If the girl is very shy, she runs out of the room; if less so, she falls on her knees and asks the blessing of her parents or guardian, as the case may be. But how is one to kneel under a tree?

Shocking! Under a tree! To be married over the broom or under a tree is just about the same thing. What a shame! What are people going to say? True enough, the marriage ceremony did not take place under a tree, but the engagement did. There is no denying it.

These were the thoughts that were troubling Madame Kriszbay. Not Veronica. She, on the contrary, was thinking that one fine day she would return to this spot with her sketch-book, and draw the old tree as a souvenir.

All this time the carriage was rolling along the dusty road. There was no room for the coachman, so he had to follow on foot, and Gyuri took the reins into his own hands, Veronica sitting on the box beside him. Oh dear! she thought, what would they think of her in the village as they drove through!

The road was better now, and they could drive faster, so Gyuri loosened the reins, and began to think over the events that had taken place. Was it a dream or not? No, it could not be, for there was Veronica sitting near to him, and behind him Father János was talking to Madame Kriszbay, torturing the language of the Gauls. No, it was simple truth, though it seemed stranger than fiction.

Who would have believed yesterday that before the sun set twice he would find his inheritance, and a wife into the bargain. Twenty-four hours ago he had not known of the existence of Miss Veronica Bélyi. Strange! And now he was trying to imagine what the world had been like without her. It seemed impossible that he had not felt the want of her yesterday. But the wheels were making such a noise that he found it difficult to think back. Wonders had happened. One legend, that of the umbrella, was done away with, but on its ruins another had built itself up. Heaven and earth had combined to help him to his inheritance. Heaven had sent a dream, and earth, or rather the precipice, a protector.

His heart swelled, boiled, exulted as he relished the thought of his happiness. Oh, if the girl next to him only knew to what a rich man she had promised her hand!

This thought rocked, elevated, tickled him, and he was silently smiling to himself like a prince in disguise, 'Just wait, till you learn the truth, my dearest.'

After passing the Kopanyicza Hills, which seem like a screen to the entrance of the valley, Glogova, with its little barrel-roofed houses, lay before them.

'We are nearly at home now,' said Veronica.

'Where is the presbytery?' asked Gyuri.

'At the other end of the village.'

'Tell me when to turn to the right or the left.'

'Very well, Mr Coachman! At present keep straight on.'

A smell of lavender pervaded the street as they drove past the familiar little gardens with their wattle fences, tall sunflowers, impaled jugs, and linen spread out to dry over the hedges. In front of the wattle gates children were playing with broken pots, and in most of the courtyards a foal was running about with a bell tied round its neck.

Otherwise the village seemed quite deserted, for all who could work were out in the fields, and the women, having cooked the dinner at home, had carried it out to their husbands. Only on the grass plot in front of the school-house was there life; there the children were at play (not all cast in the same mould now as in schoolmaster Majzik's younger days); there were fair and dark ones now, straight-haired and curly-headed, and their greetings to those in the carriage were in Hungarian.

Of the villagers only the 'aristocratic' were at home. Waving his hat at the threshold of a pretty little stone house with tiled roof stood Mr Gongoly, much stouter than some years before. To judge by his paunch he might have spent the last ten years in gaol. (Peasants as a rule only get fat in prison.) In front of the smithy sat Klincsok, quietly smoking, whilst the smith mended a wheel.

'Hallo!' he called out, wildly gesticulating. 'So you've come back! Why, we were thinking of looking out for another priest!' Which showed that Father János's absence had been noticed.

How Glogova had changed in the last few years! Farther up, on the hill behind the Krizsáns' house, there glistened the new Calvary with its twelve steps, and there was a slender tower to the church too, the like of which was not to be seen except in Losoncz; only that on the tower of Losoncz there was a weather-cock. In the middle of the village was an inn, 'The Miraculous Umbrella', with Virginia creeper climbing all over it, and near it a pretty little white house, looking as though it were made of sugar; behind it a garden, with iron railings, and a soldierly row of young white poplars in front.

'Whose house is that?' asked Gyuri, turning round.

'The owner is on the box-seat beside you.'

'Really? Is it yours, Veronica?'

She nodded her head, blushing.

'There is a small farm belonging to it,' said Father János modestly.

'Well, we won't take it with us, but leave it here for your brother, shall we, Veronica?' said Gyuri disparagingly.

Then he turned to the priest again, saying:

'Veronica has a fortune worthy of a countess, but neither you nor she knows of it.'

But the priest and Veronica were so surprised at this announcement that they did not notice they were in front of the presbytery, and Gyuri would have driven on if Vistula, the old watchdog, had not rushed out barking with joy, and old Widow Adamecz called out, with the tears rolling down her face:

'Holy Mary! you have heard the prayers of your servant!'

'Stop! here we are. Open the gate, Mrs Adamecz.'

The widow wiped away her tears, dropped her rosary, and got up to open the gate.

'Is dinner ready?' asked Father János.

'Dinner? Of course not. Whom was I to cook for? We all thought your reverence was lost. I have not even lighted the fire, for my tears would only have put it out again.'

'Never mind, Mrs Adamecz. I feel sure you were anxious on my account, but now go and see about some dinner for us, for we are dying of hunger.'

Veronica had become suspicious at the widow's words, and began to storm her brother with questions; then burst out crying and turned her back upon Gyuri, declaring they were hiding something from her. So they were obliged to tell her the truth, and her poor little heart nearly broke when she thought of what her brother had gone through, and what danger he had been in.

Whilst this was going on, Mrs Adamecz was bustling about in the kitchen, and giving everyone plenty of work to do. Both the maids were called in to help, and the farm servant too.

'Come and whip this cream, Hanka. And you, Borbála, go and fetch some salt. Is the goose plucked? Oh, you lazy-bones. Quick, András, run and pick some parsley in the garden. Dear me! How very thin the good lady is whom Miss Veronica has brought home with her. Did you see her? I shall have hard work to feed her up and make her decently fat. Give me a saucepan; not that one, the other. And, Borbála, grate me some bread-crumbs. But the young man is handsome. I wonder where he comes from? What he wants here? What did you say? You don't know? of course you don't know, silly, if I don't. But this much is certain (between ourselves, of course), there is something strange in Miss Veronica's eyes. Something has happened, I'll be hanged if it hasn't, but I can't make out what.'

Widow Adamecz chattered of all sorts of things, both good and bad, but her cooking was excellent, and she gave them such a dinner that even the lovers found their appetites.

After dinner, Gyuri sent a man on horseback with a letter to Mr Sztolarik in Besztercebánya.

My Dear Guardian,

I have great things to communicate to you, but at present can only write the outlines, the rest I shall tell you personally. I have found the umbrella, partly through Mrs Müncz, partly by chance. At present I am in Glogova, at the priest's house, whose sister Veronica I have asked in marriage. She is a very pretty girl, besides there is no way of getting at the money unless I marry her. Special circumstances have cropped up. Please send me by the messenger two gold rings from Sámuel Huszák's shop, and the certificate of my birth; it must be amongst your papers somewhere. I should like the banns to be published the day after tomorrow.

I remain, etc.

He told the messenger to hurry.

'I'll hurry, but the horse won't!'

'Well, use your spurs.'

'So I would, but there are no spurs on sandals!'

The Slovak had had a wretched horse, but Time had a fast one. A day had flashed by like a minute and next day they heard a carriage stop at the door, and who should get out but Sztolarik himself. Great man though he was, no one was glad to see him except the priest. Veronica felt frightened. She hardly knew why, but it seemed as though a breath of cold air had entered with him. Why had he come here just now?

But the old lawyer was very pleasant to her.

'So this is little Veronica?' he asked.

'Yes,' answered Gyuri proudly. (How much triumphant pride goes into a word of one syllable!)

The old gentleman took her small hand in his large one, and pinched her cheek in fatherly fashion. But no amount of pinching would bring the roses back just then. Her heart was heavy with fear. Why, oh why had he come?

Gyuri was surprised, too, for Sztolarik hated to leave his home.

'Have you brought them?' he asked.

'Yes.'

Veronica drew a breath of relief, for Gyuri had mentioned that he expected the engagement rings from Besztercebánya.

'Give them to me,' he said.

'Later on,' answered the old lawyer. 'First of all I must speak to you.'

He must speak to him first? Then he must have something to say which could not be said after they had exchanged rings! Veronica again felt a weight on her heart. Gyuri got up reluctantly from his place next to Veronica, whose fingers began to play nervously with the work she had in her hands.

'Come across to my room then.'

Gyuri's room was at the other end of the house, which was built in the shape of an L. It used to be the schoolroom before the new school was built. (Widow Adamecz had learned her ABC there.) The priest who had been there before Father János had divided the big room into two parts by a nicely painted wooden partition, and of one half he had made a spare bedroom, of the other a store-room.

Veronica was feeling as miserable as she could, and her one wish at the moment was to hear the two gentlemen's conversation, for everything depended on that. Some demon who had evidently never been to a convent school, and had never learnt that it was dishonourable to listen at doors or walls, whispered to her:

'Run quickly, Veronica, into the store-room, and if you press your ear secretly to the thin wall, you will be able to hear what they say.'

Off went Veronica like a shot. It is incredible what an amount of honey a demon of that description can put into his words; he was capable of persuading this well-educated girl to take her place amongst the pickled cucumbers, basins of lard, and sacks of potatoes, in order to listen intently to a conversation which was not meant for her ears.

Not a sound was to be heard in the store-room, but the throbbing of her heart and the dripping of the fat from a side of bacon hanging from the rafters, and which the great heat there was causing to melt. Some of it even fell on her pretty dress, but what did she care for that just then?

'So you have found out all about the umbrella,' she heard Sztolarik say, 'but have you seen it yet?'

'Why should I?' asked Gyuri. 'I cannot touch its contents till after the wedding.'

'Why not sooner?'

'Because, for various reasons, I do not wish the story of the umbrella known.'

'For instance?'

'First of all, because Father János would be the laughing-stock of the place.'

'Why do you trouble your head about the priest?'

'Secondly, because it would give Veronica reason to think I am only marrying her for the sake of the umbrella.'

'But she will know it later on in any case.'

'I shall never tell her.'

'Have you any other reasons?'

'Oh yes, I daresay they would not even give me the cheque; it is probably not made out in any particular name, so how am I to prove to them that it is mine? It really belongs to the person who has it in his possession. And perhaps they would not even give me the girl, for if her fortune is as large as we think it, she can find as many husbands as she has fingers on her hands.'

Veronica felt giddy. It was as though they were driving nails into her flesh. She could not quite understand all they were talking about—of umbrellas, cheques, large fortunes. What fortune? But this much she had begun to understand, that she was only the means to some unfathomable, mysterious end.

'Well, well,' began Sztolarik again after a short pause, 'the affair seems to be pretty entangled at present, but there is still worse to come.'

'What more can come?' asked Gyuri in an uncertain voice.

'Don't you ask anything at present. The five o'clock train has not arrived yet. Let us find out first of all whether you love the girl.'

Poor little Veronica was trembling like a shivering bird in her hiding-place. She shut her eyes like a condemned person might do when laying his neck on the block, in a sort of unreasonable expectation that the blow would be less painful so. What would he answer?

'I think I love her,' answered Gyuri, again in that uncertain voice. 'She is so pretty, don't you think so?'

'Of course. There is nothing wrong with my eyesight either. But the question is, would you in other circumstances have asked her to marry you? Answer frankly!'

'I should never have thought of such a thing.'

A shriek was heard in the next room, and then a noise as though some pieces of furniture had been thrown down.

Sztolarik listened for a few moments, and then, pointing to the wall, asked:

'Do you know what is on the other side?'

'I think it is the store-room.'

'I thought I heard someone shriek.'

'Perhaps one of the servants saw a mouse.'

And that is how a tragedy looks from the next room, when the wall is thin. If there is a thick wall, it does not even seem so bad. One of the servants had seen a mouse, or a heart had been broken; for who was to know that utter despair and silly fright only have one sound to express them?

Veronica, with the thorn that had pierced her heart, ran out into the open air; she wished to hear no more, only to get away from that hated place, for she felt suffocating; away, away, as far as she could go . . . And this all seemed, from the next room, as though Widow Adamecz or Hanka had seen a mouse. But however it may have seemed to them, they had forgotten the whole thing in half a minute, so deeply engrossed they were in the subject of their conversation.

'You say it would never have occurred to you to marry her. So you had better not hurry with the rings and even less so with the wedding. Let us first see the umbrella and its contents, and then we shall see what is to be done next.'

Gyuri went on quietly smoking his cigarette and thought:

'Sztolarik is getting old. Fancy making such a fuss about it!'

'I have thought it well over,' he went on aloud, trying to be tactful, 'and there is no other way of managing it; I must marry the girl.'

Sztolarik got up from his chair, and came and stood in front of the young man, fixing his slyly winking eyes on him, all set for firing his main argument.

'But supposing you could get at your inheritance without marrying Veronica?'

Gyuri could not help smiling.

'Why, I have just said,' he exclaimed impatiently, 'that it cannot be done, but even if it could, I would not do it, for I feel as though she also had a right to the fortune as it has been in her possession so long, and Providence seems to have sent it direct to her.'

'But supposing you could not get at it through Veronica?'

'That seems out of the question too.'

'Really? Well, now listen to me, Gyuri, for the five o'clock train I referred to before is about to rattle in.'

'I am listening.'

But his thoughts were elsewhere, as he drummed on the table with his fingers.

'Well,' went on Sztolarik, 'when I went in to Huszák's this morning to buy the two rings you wanted sent by the messenger (for I had no intention of coming here myself then), the goldsmith was not in his shop, so it was József Klaniczay, his journeyman, the rabbit-mouthed young man, that waited on me. You know him?'

Yes, Gyuri remembered him.

'I told him to give me two rings, and he asked whom they were for. So I said they were going a good distance. Then he asked where to, and I told him to Glogova. "Perhaps to the priest's sister?" he asked. "Yes," I said. "She's a beauty," he remarked. "Why, do you know her?" asked I. "Very well," he answered.'

Gyuri stopped tapping, and jumped up excitedly.

'Did he say anything about Veronica?'

'You shall hear in a minute. Whilst he was wrapping up the rings he went on talking. How had he got to know the priest's sister? "I was in Glogova last year." "And what the devil were you doing in Glogova?" "Why, the villagers were having a silver handle made here for a wretched-looking old umbrella which they keep in their church, and the stupid things were afraid to send the umbrella here for fear anyone should steal it, though it was not worth twopence; so I was obliged to go there in order to fasten the handle on".'

'Why, this is dreadful!' exclaimed Gyuri turning pale.

Sztolarik smiled knowingly.

'That is only why I said, my friend, that we had better wait a bit before deciding anything.'

'Let us go at once to Father János and ask him to show us the umbrella.'

He could not wait a minute longer. He had been so near to his object, and now it was slipping from him again, like a Fata Morgana, which lures the wanderer on to look for it.

It was easy to find the priest; he was feeding his pigeons in the garden.

'Father János,' began Gyuri, 'now Mr Sztolarik is here, he would like to look at your wonderful umbrella. Can we see it?'

'Of course. Mrs Adamecz,' he called out to the old woman who was plucking a fowl at the kitchen-door. 'Will you bring me out the key of the church, please?'

She did as she was asked, and the priest, going on in front, led his visitors through the church between the rows of time-blackened pews under the cool arches of the vaulted roof.

How beautiful those shabby village churches are, and everything that belongs to them. The lawn round the church, the red, green and other banners inside, with the pictures of gentle, beautiful women on them: '*Santa Barbara, Santa Rosalia, ora pro nobis.*'

How many legends within reach! The inhabitants of Heaven brought down half way (for the church is half way to Heaven) to be together with mortals. Facing the door stands the high altar with the image of St Nicholas, the former patron saint of Glogova. (I say 'former', since for some time now he had been losing ground to St Peter.) To the left, above the aspersorium, the image of Christ before which young Father János knelt in prayer on that famous day when Máté Billeghi had brought Veronica, the little orphan, to Glogova. Everything here is quiet and sublime, the bleak walls breathe peace and divine grace, the smell of frankincense, mingled with the odour of the flowers the flaxen-haired Glogova girls brought with them Sunday last, still lingers in the air turning somersaults on the bright shaft of sunlight that steals through an upper window.

Everything here has a story to it; the fine, thick wax-candles were presented to God by Mrs Domanyik when He took her husband away: tit for tat you would think, but would be wrong, for the embroidered altar-cloth is the work of Mrs Gongoly, who was later on drowned for all that, which shows that God cannot be bribed.

'This way, gentlemen, into the sacristy.'

As they stepped in, there it was before them! From among the chasubles, pluvials and stoles Pál Gregorics's old umbrella smiled at them, and seemed like an old friend, only the handle, yes, the handle, was unknown to them, for it was of silver.

Gyuri gazed at it speechlessly, and felt that fate was against him. A demon was behind him, constantly urging him on, and whispering, 'Go on, go on, and look for your inheritance!' A second demon ran on before him, beckoning and crying, 'Come along, it is this way!'

But there was a third one, the liveliest of all, who followed in the wake of the second one, and each time Gyuri thought he had attained his end, this demon turned round and laughed in his face, saying, 'There is nothing here!'

Sztolarik kept his countenance, and carefully examined the handle of the umbrella, as though he were admiring the work.

'Had it always this same handle?' he asked.

'Oh dear, no, this is of solid silver, and very finely chased. The goldsmith in Besztercebánya made it, and he is quite an artist. Just look at the style, and what taste is displayed in it. My parishioners had it made last summer as a surprise for me, whilst I was away at the baths in Szklenó. The old handle had been broken off, and it was almost impossible to make use of the umbrella. I expect it was Klincsok's idea, for he started the collection. There are still plenty of good Christian hearts to be found.'

Then he turned to Gyuri.

'I will introduce you to Klincsok, he is a very worthy man.'

Gyuri wished the worthy Klincsok in hell, and he could even have found him a companion for the journey, for behind him was the first demon, again, whispering, 'Go and look for your inheritance!'

'But I suppose they kept the old handle?' he asked.

'I do not think so,' answered the priest. 'It was only of common wood; I believe Mrs Adamecz asked Veronica for it.'

(It must have been the second demon speaking through the priest, 'The handle of the umbrella is in Mrs Adamecz's possession.')

Sztolarik now became curious, too.

'Who is Mrs Adamecz?' he asked.

'My old cook, who just now brought me the keys.'

Mr Sztolarik burst out laughing, the walls of the empty church re-echoing with the sound. When they were outside, and the priest had gone in with the keys, the old lawyer took the two rings out of the paper they were wrapped in and pressed them into Gyuri's palm, saying quaintly:

'According to your logic of half an hour ago, you must now marry old Mrs Adamecz, so go and ask for her hand at once.'

Gyuri gave no answer to this cruel thrust and rushed nervously into the kitchen, where the widow was just frying pancakes.

'I say, Mrs Adamecz, where have you put the old handle of the church umbrella?'

Widow Adamecz finished frying her pancake, put it warily on a wooden platter with those she had already fried, and then turned round to see who was speaking to her.

'What have I done with the old handle, my dear? Well, you see, this is how it was. My little grandson, Matykó, got ill last year just at cabbage-cutting time, no, I believe it was earlier in the year . . .'

'I don't care when it was, only go on.'

Widow Adamecz quietly poured some more of the batter into the frying-pan.

'Let me see, what was I saying? Ah, yes, I was speaking of Matykó. Well, it was the result of the evil eye. A beauty of a child, Matykó is . . .'

(The peasants think that if a child is much looked at and enviously admired, it pines away.)

Gyuri began impatiently to tap with his foot on the floor.

'Will you tell me where it is?'

'It is there, under the table.'

'What, the handle?'

'No, the child.'

Yes, there was Matykó, squatting on a basin turned upside down, a fat-faced, blue-eyed Slovak child, playing with some dried beans, its face still dirty from the pancakes it had eaten.

'Bother you, woman! Are you deaf?' burst out the lawyer. 'I asked you about the handle of the umbrella, not about the child.'

Mrs Adamecz tossed her head indignantly.

'Well, that's just what I am talking about. I tell you, they cast an evil eye on Matykó, and the poor little angel was fading away. There is only one remedy for that: you must take a burning stick, and let three sparks fall from it into a glass of water, and of this the child must drink for three days. I did this, but it was of no use; the child went on suffering and getting thinner from day to day, and my heart nearly broke at the sight of him; for I have a very soft heart, as his reverence will tell you . . .'

'I don't doubt it for a minute, but for heaven's sake answer my question.'

'I am coming to it in a minute, sir. Just at that time they were having the silver handle made to the umbrella, and our young lady, pretty dear, gave me the old handle. Why, thought I, that will be just the thing for Matykó; if three sparks from that holy wood are of no use, then Matykó will be entered in the ranks of God's soldiers.'

At the thought of little Matykó as one of God's soldiers her tears began to flow. It was lucky if none of them fell into the frying-pan.

'Mrs Adamecz!' exclaimed Gyuri, alarmed, his voice trembling. 'You surely did not burn the handle?'

The old woman looked at him surprised.

'How was I to get the three sparks from it if I did not burn it?'

Gyuri fell back against the wall, the kitchen and everything in it swam before his eyes, the plates, pots and basins seemed to be dancing a waltz together; a tongue of fire arose from the fire-place, bringing with it the third demon, who exclaimed, 'There is nothing here!'

But all at once he felt a hand laid on his arm. It was Sztolarik.

'It was, and is no more,' he said. 'But never mind. Fate intended it to be so. For the future you will not at all events run after a shadow, you will be yourself again, and that is worth a good deal, after all.'

-III-

Little Veronica is Taken Away

But it was of no use Sztolarik preaching about the uselessness of wordly goods, for those wordly goods are very pleasant to have.

When a favourite child dies, there always is a wise member of the family who, trying to comfort the anguished hearts of the parents, will say such things as, 'Who knows how the child would have turned out? It might have come to the gallows in time; perhaps it was better it had died now,' and the like. But for all that, wisdom has never yet dried a single tear. Words, however wise, are poor consolation.

Sztolarik said all he could think of to console Gyuri, but the young lawyer was quite cast down at the thought that his dreams would never now be realized; his whole life before him looked dark and threatening. But the world was the same as of old, and everything went on just the same as though Widow Adamecz had never burnt the handle of the umbrella.

The hands of the parish clock pointed to the Roman figure II, and the chimes rang out on the air; the servants laid the table for dinner, Mrs Adamecz brought in the soup, and his reverence led his guests into the dining-room, and placed them right and left of Madame Kriszbay, when all at once they noticed that Veronica was missing.

'I was just going to ask,' said Madame Kriszbay, 'if she had been with the gentlemen?'

'I thought she was with you,' said the priest.

'I have not seen her for two hours.'

'Nor I.'

'Nor we.'

'Perhaps she is in the kitchen?'

Madame Kriszbay looked vexed, got up from her seat, and went into the kitchen to call her pupil, but returned at once with the remark that she had not been seen there either.

'Where can she be?' exclaimed the priest annoyed, and ran out to look for her, sending the servants to some of her favourite seats in the garden, thinking she might have gone there to read, and have forgotten the time.

Mrs Adamecz grumbled in the kitchen, for the dinner was spoiling.

'Well, serve the dinner,' said Father János, for, of course, he could not keep his guests waiting, especially as Sztolarik wanted to return home as soon as possible.

So the dishes were brought in one after the other, goose with rice, stuffed cabbage, roast pork, and pancakes—a meal worthy of a king—but still there was no sign of Veronica; and Hanka had returned with the news that no one had seen her.

Gyuri sat in his place, pale and quiet.

'Perhaps she is in the apiary,' suggested her brother, 'or perhaps (here he hesitated a minute, not knowing how to continue), perhaps something unpleasant has taken place between you?'

And he fixed his eyes inquiringly on the lawyer.

Gyuri looked up embarrassed.

'Nothing has taken place between us,' he said coldly.

'Then Hanka, run across to the new house and look in the apiary. Please excuse her, gentlemen, she is such a child still, and follows her own whims. She is probably chasing a butterfly. Take some more wine, Mr Sztolarik.'

He was trying to reassure himself, not his guests, as he sat there listening to every sound, paying scant attention to the conversation, and giving many wrong answers.

Sztolarik asked if the bad weather this year had made much difference to the harvest.

'I don't know.'

'Have you any other brothers or sisters?'

'I had one or two,' answered the priest.

His replies showed the perturbed state of his mind, and it was only for the sake of decency he kept his seat at table. At length, when coffee had been served, the old lawyer said:

'Perhaps it would be better if your reverence were to go and look for Miss Veronica yourself; and I should be glad if you would send word to my coachman that I wish to start as soon as possible, for it is a long drive to Besztercebánya.'

The priest seized the opportunity, and begging Madame Kriszbay to excuse him, hurried away, for he found Veronica's absence very strange, and was beginning to get anxious. So, Madame Kriszbay having retired, the two gentlemen were left alone, and a painful silence ensued to which the incessant ticking of the grandfather's clock furnished a ghastly undertone. Gyuri was gazing with melancholy eyes at the canary which, perching on a rod in its cage, was also silent now.

'You had better order your carriage, too,' said Sztolarik, breaking the silence at last. 'We could leave at the same time.'

Gyuri murmured some unintelligible answer, and shook his head, which made it clear that he had no intention to go.

'But you will have to leave soon, for our part here is played out.'

'I tell you it is impossible.'

'Why?'

'Don't you see that Veronica is lost?'

'What does that matter to you? The umbrella handle is lost, too.'

Gyuri made an impatient gesture, upsetting a couple of glasses.

'What do I care about the umbrella!'

'So it is the girl you want? You told me a different tale before dinner.'

Gyuri turned round.

'I did not know then.'

'And now you know?'

'Yes, now I know,' he answered curtly.

'And may I ask,' said Sztolarik acidly, 'when did Amor light this flaming fire? For the girl's disappearance does not seem to prove that she cares.'

'And yet it is causing me at the present moment all the tortures of hell. Believe me, my dear guardian, the loss of my inheritance seems to me a trifle beside the loss of Veronica.'

Sztolarik was impressed by the apparent sincerity of Gyuri's sorrow.

'That's quite another thing,' he said. 'If that is how you feel, I will stay here with you. Let us go and look for the girl ourselves, and find out what she thinks on the subject.'

When they went out, they found a great confusion reigning in the courtyard, but Mrs Adamecz was loudest in her lamentations.

'I knew this would be the end of it. A fairy should never be touched by a mortal's hand, or she will dissolve in thin air. Oh, our dear young lady! She was God's bride, and they wanted to make her the bride of a mortal, so God has taken her to Himself.'

Sztolarik sprang towards her, and caught hold of her hand.

'What is that you say? Have you heard anything?'

'Mrs Gundros, the cow-herd's wife, has just told us that she saw our young lady this morning running straight towards the Biela Voda, across the meadows, and her eyes were red, as though she had been crying. There is only one conclusion to be drawn from that.'

A lot of women and children were gathered round the kitchen-door, and one of them had also seen Veronica earlier than Mrs Gundros had.

'Did she look sad?' asked Gyuri.

'She was crying.'

'Oh dear!' exclaimed Gyuri despairingly.

'We will look for her,' Sztolarik assured him.

'Where?'

'Out in the meadows, for it is certain she must be somewhere there, and we shall soon find her.'

'That will not be so easy,' sighed Gyuri, 'for we have no glass to show us things as they have in fairy-tales.'

'I'll have the whole village round us in a few minutes.'

Gyuri shook his head doubtfully. Had Sztolarik gone mad to think he could call all the people together from the fields, from the woods, from everywhere round about? But the old lawyer was as good as his word. Veronica must be found at any cost.

'Where is his reverence?' he asked of the bystanders.

'He has gone to the pond where the hemp is soaked, to see if the young lady has fallen in there.'

'Where is the bell-ringer?'

'Here I am, sir.'

'Go up at once into the tower, and ring the big bell.'

'But there is no fire!'

'That does not matter. If I order it to be done, you must do it. Do you know me?'

Of course he knew Mr Sztolarik, who had often been to Glogova as county magistrate, before he had been made President of the Courts. So off ran Pál Kvapka, and in a few minutes the big fire-bell was tolling. There was no wind, and the sound was carried for miles around over the meadows, into the woods, over the mountains, and soon the people came running up from every side. It was astonishing how soon the villagers were assembled round the presbytery. Those who saw it will never see its like again, until the Archangel Gabriel sounds his trumpet at the last day.

Sztolarik gazed placidly at the breathless, panting crowd assembled around him.

'Now,' he said, 'I have only to stand up in their midst and ask them if any of them have seen Veronica. But it will be quite unnecessary, for Veronica herself will soon be here. Look out of the window,' he called up to the bell-ringer, 'and tell me if you can see the young lady.'

'Yes, I can see her, she is running through the Srankós' maize-field.'

'She lives!' exclaimed Gyuri ecstatically, but his joy was soon at an end, for he thought, 'If there is nothing the matter with her, she must have run away from me.'

And he began to wonder if it would not have been better if she were dead, for then he could have believed she loved him, and could have loved her and sorrowed for her.

The bell-ringer still went on tolling the bell, so Sztolarik called up to him:

'Stop tolling, you fool, can't you? Show us which way the Srankós' maize-field lies.'

The bell-ringer pointed to the right.

'You run on in front, Gyuri, and try and get out of her what is the matter with her.'

But Gyuri was already gone, through the priest's garden, across Magát's clover-field, and his heart began to beat, for from there he could see Veronica in her green dress, without a hat, only a little red silk shawl round her shoulders. Across Szlávik's corn-field, then into Gongoly's meadow, and they were face to face.

The girl drew a sobbing breath when she saw him, and began to tremble violently.

'Where is the fire?' she asked.

'Don't be frightened, there is no fire. My guardian had the bell rung so as to make you return home. Why did you run away?'

The girl turned pale, and bit her lip.

'It is enough if I know the reason,' she said in a low voice. 'Please leave me alone.'

And she turned round as though to return to the woods.

'Veronica, for Heaven's sake, don't torture me; what have I done?'

The girl looked at him coldly, her eyes were like two bits of ice.

'Leave me alone,' she said, 'what do you want with me?'

The young man caught hold of her hand, and Veronica did her best to free herself from his grasp, but he would not let go her hand till he had forced a ring on to her finger.

- 214 -

'That is what I want,' he said.

'That is what you want, is it?' laughed the girl bitterly. 'And this is what I want!' And she tore off the ring and threw it away, across the meadow, into the grass. Poor Gyuri fell back a few steps.

'Oh!' he exclaimed, 'why did you do it? Why?'

'Do not try to deceive me any longer, Mr Wibra. You should not put a ring on my finger, but on the umbrella, for that is what you really want to marry.'

Gyuri began to understand what had taken place.

'Good Heavens! You listened to our conversation!'

'Yes, I know all!' said Veronica, blushing slightly. 'It is no good your denying it.'

'I don't wish to deny anything. But listen to me, please.'

They walked quietly through the meadow, Gyuri talking, the girl listening, whilst the thousands of insects which peopled the fields flew away before their feet. Gyuri related the story of his life, and of his father's, of the supposed inheritance, of his search for it, and how he had gathered the threads together till they led him to Bábaszék. In short, he told her everything. The girl listened to him, first with reproach in her eyes, then as a judge, trying to find out the truth, and as the story began to interest her more and more, she became quite excited. Now she was neither plaintiff nor judge, only an interested listener, surprised that the threads led nearer and nearer to herself. Now Gyuri is speaking of Mrs Müncz's son, now Móricz is telling his story, which shows that the umbrella must be in Glogova. Then the forester's wife tells the tale of St Peter's bringing the umbrella to the orphan child. A few more words and the story was complete.

Veronica knew all, and her eyes were swimming in tears.

'Oh dear, how dreadful! Mrs Adamecz burned the handle!'

'God bless her for it!' said Gyuri brightly, seeing the change of the girl's heart, 'for now at least I can prove to you that I love you for yourself, alone.'

Veronica had taken off the small red shawl and was swinging it in her hand. Suddenly she caught hold of Gyuri's arm, and smiled at him through her tears.

'Do you really mean that you still want to marry me?'

'Of course. What do you say to it?'

'I say that . . .' She ceased speaking, for there was a strange feeling in her throat.

'Well?'

'That you are very volatile, and . . .'

'And?'

'And that . . . Let us run back and look for my ring.'

With that she turned, and ran as fast as she could to the part of the meadow in which they had been standing when she threw the ring away. Gyuri could hardly keep up with her.

They looked for the ring a long time, but it was not to be found. And soon Father János appeared on the scene.

'I say, Gyuri, don't say anything about the umbrella to my brother.'

'No, my darling, I will never mention it.'

His reverence gave Veronica a good scolding.

'You naughty girl! Is that the way to behave? How you frightened us! Of course, you were chasing a butterfly?'

'No, I was running away from one, but it caught me.'

'What, the butterfly?'

'Yes, that ugly, big butterfly standing beside you.'

His reverence understood as much as he was meant to, and set to work too, to look for the ring. But they might have looked for it till Doomsday if pot-bellied Mr Gongoly had not passed that way. Veronica had quite despaired of finding the ring.

'Well, well, my dear,' said the nabob of Glogova, shaking back his long grey hair, which was held together by a comb at the back, 'never mind, trust in Gongoly, he will find it for you. There is a way to do it. Reading mass is one thing, finding the ring is another. In an hour's time they will be making hay in this field.'

Though the grass was not two inches high (it had only been cut a fortnight before), Mr Gongoly sent his men there to mow it, with the result that next day the ring was safely resting on Veronica's finger. And for years the people spoke of the wonderful fact that in that year gallant Mr Gongoly's meadow gave three crops of hay, and it was always mentioned if anyone spoke disparagingly of the Glogova fields.

What more am I to say? I think there still would be plenty to tell. All the same, there are some things that will never be known for certain; for instance, what really became of Pál Gregorics's fortune, for there is no sign of it to this day. Was the supposed receipt in the handle of the umbrella or not? No one will ever know, not even little Matykó, who drank at least three sparks of it. No king drinks such precious liquid as he did—if the story be true.

The legend of St Peter's holy umbrella is still believed in, in those parts. Mr Sztolarik, who was fond of a plain fact, certainly told the true version of the story, how old Müncz the Jew had made a present to Christianity of a holy relic, and so on; but belief was stronger than truth and it gradually buried the latter. I for one don't want to dig it up, and apologize for having attempted to do so. And after all, there really was something mystic and strange in the whole affair, and the umbrella had brought worldly goods to everyone, Gyuri included, for it had given him the dearest little wife in the world.

They were married very soon, and never had such a wedding taken place in Glogova before. According to Veronica's special wish, everyone who had been at the Mravucsáns' supper was invited to the wedding, for she wanted all those who had been present at their first meeting to take part in their happiness. There were a lot of guests from Besztercebánya, too, amongst them the mother of the bridegroom, in a black silk dress, the President of the Courts, the mayor, and lots of others. Then there were the Urszinyis from Kopanyica, two young ladies from Lehota in accordion-pleated pink skirts, and Mrs Müncz from Bábaszék with golden ear-rings on as big as my fist.

There were so many different kinds of conveyances in Glogova that day, it would have taken a week to look at them all. After evensong, the sacristan quickly ushered out the peasants, but the priest stayed on, to receive the wedding-guests.

Dear me, what a lovely procession it was, too; all gentlefolk clad in the finest cloth and silk. They walked in pairs, a lady beside a gentleman, a young lady beside a young man. At the head of the procession walked the bride in a lovely white dress with a long veil and a wreath of orange blossoms. (Oh, how pretty she was! A pity she, too, would grow old one day!)

But the bridegroom was splendid, too, in the same kind of attire in which the king has his portrait painted sometimes. His sword, in a velvet sheath mounted in gold, clattered on the pavement as he walked up the church.

They stood in a semicircle round the altar, each lady with a nosegay of flowers in her hand, and perfumed to such an extent that the church smelt like a perfumer's shop.

It was a little cool in the church, and the young ladies from Lehota, always of indifferent health, were seen to shiver now and then in their thin pink dresses; but everything went off very well.

The bridegroom spoke his 'yes' in a loud firm voice the walls seemed to re-echo, but the bride spoke it almost in a whisper, it sounded like the buzzing of a fly.

Poor child! She got so nervous towards the end of the ceremony that she began to cry. Then she looked for her handkerchief, but was there ever a pocket in a wedding-dress? She could not find it, so someone from behind offered her one, then turned and said:

'Button up your coat, Wladin!'